FINDING PURPOSE

Colorado Veterans Book 1

TIFFANI LYNN

COPYRIGHT

DEDICATION

For retired Master Sergeant Bernard I. Morrin USAF, my father and the proudest veteran I've ever known. Thank you for your dedicated service and for teaching me to have pride in our country and respect for those who serve in the armed forces. Having a dad in the military wasn't always easy but it gave me some great memories and amazing friends. I'm proud of you and will love you always.

ACKNOWLEDGMENTS

The first bit of gratitude goes out to my amazing husband and three fantastic daughters. Your pride and encouragement have helped me to keep writing and sharing my words with the reading world. Teddy you've given me my happily ever after and I love living the dream with you.

Thank you to the incredibly talented photographer Michael Stokes. Always Loyal is what started my thoughts churning for this story and introduced me to the beauty of B.T. Urruela and Redmond Ramos. These two men were the inspiration for the hero in this story. B.T. and Redmond, thank you for sharing your stories and your scars with us. Your strength, courage and smiles are an inspiration.

I'd like to express my gratitude to Kelsey Imig Huber, a former member of the Ohio State University Varsity Pistol Team and the muse for my heroine. Although the direction the story took wasn't what I originally intended, I enjoyed getting to know the woman behind the character's inspiration. It wasn't until I sent several emails with a ton of questions that I realized she wasn't only tough but also cool, patient and kind. The world needs more women like you Kelsey. Thank you.

John and Marcia Migacz meeting you was such a blessing. Your open and honest conversation gave me helpful insight I couldn't find anywhere else. I look forward to more laughs and a lasting friendship. I wish you both much success!

Rachel Javier, thank you so much for sharing your nursing knowledge with me and for all the extra reading you've done. You've been a huge help to me.

Special thanks to Mia Sparks for running my street team and for helping me with so many different things. You have such a giving heart and I appreciate you more than you know.

The support and love from my TLC family is irreplaceable. Much love and gratitude to all of you. As always, what you find is what you find!

Judy Swinson, Kat Mizera, Katharina LeBoeuf, Lexi Post and Sam JD Hunt, y'all have each helped me in one way or another and I appreciate all of your support, encouragement and assistance.

Finally, I'll never tire of thanking my Beta Babes. Alison Dye, April Klusman, Barb Teeter, Barbie Stokes Timpson, Gemma Blomquist, Jackie Ziegler, Judy Swinson, Kat Mizera, Lisa Qualls, Maria Robinette, Rachel Garcia, Rachel Javier and Terri Kuebbeler if I had a million dollars for each of you it still wouldn't come close to your worth.

Chapter One

JUDSON

EVERYTHING IS BLACK. I struggle to open my eyes as the pain barrels through me from head to toe. Burning, aching, stomach turning pain. My hands, my leg and my side hurt so badly I want to hurl. In an instant, memories flood my brain of the explosion and I call out, "Jackson, Barker, you okay?!" No answer. I panic and scream for them but only hear murmured voices to my right. *Why can't I open my eyes?* The voices are feminine, not what my guys sound like. Where are Jackson and Barker? As the pain flares through me at an alarming rate my focus on finding the guys fades and I struggle just to open my eyes. I've got to get my bearings, I can't get out of this if I don't know where the hell I am. No matter how hard I try they simply won't open. The pain is surreal, unlike anything I've ever felt before or thought a body could feel.

Finally, I pry my eyes open and am stunned at what I see. From the angle I'm at it looks like I'm in the hospital, but the blurry vision makes this appear like a dream. Please let that be the case so I can wake up and be out of this literal burning hell. The clearer my eyes become the more the pain intensifies. *Holy fuck!* I didn't think the pain could get worse. Even through SEAL training it never got this bad and that was horrific.

"Judson, oh my God, Judson. You're awake. How do you feel? Are you okay? What do you need?" My heart rate picks up, galloping like a runaway horse as Quincy Hannigan steps into my line of sight though fuzzy around the edges. This has to be a dream. I haven't seen her in years. Not since I left her standing outside her dorm crying as I pulled away. I blink rapidly, trying to clear the blurriness further out of the way. *Fuck, fuck, fuck.* I can't concentrate on why Quinn's here because I hurt all over. *Please make it stop.*

"Call the nurse and tell her he's awake," I hear Quinn say urgently.

Someone else responds in a deep familiar voice but I can't quite place it. I attempt to sit up but the pain is all-encompassing so I fall back and cry out. I've got to be dying or already dead or this is the worst dream I've ever had. *Why do I hurt so badly? If that explosion was real, I'd be dead. This has to be a dream. Please, please, please let this be a dream.* If Quinn's here it has to be a dream. Now I need to figure out how to wake up from it.

Quinn's voice is back. *Focus on the voice.* I always loved the sound of her voice. Maybe if I focus on that the rest will fade.

"Judson, the nurse will get you something for the pain. Just hold on for a few minutes. The Colonel has gone to get someone." Her fingers touch the over-sensitized skin of my forearm and I cry out again.

What the hell is going on?! How bad is it?

"Oh God, Judson. I'm sorry. I didn't mean to hurt you." I can hear the tears in her voice and that's almost as bad as the pain. If this is a dream, I need to wake up soon. *Dear God, if I'm dying please let me go now.*

Another voice joins in, this one unfamiliar, high-pitched and slightly annoying so I clench my eyes shut, not caring who it is. "Chief Rivers, can you hear me?" the annoying voice asks. I try to nod, hoping I am. "Chief Rivers, are you in pain?" I try to nod again.

"I'm going to press the button on his PCA pump for his morphine. If you know he's in pain, you can hit it the next time. He won't be able to do it because his hands are bandaged. It's this button right here."

My hands are bandaged?

"I don't want to hit it too many times and OD him. If he's in pain, I'll just keep hitting it to take that away. I can't stand to see him like this." Her voice shakes and even after all these years I can still tell when she's on the verge of tears.

"You won't. It's set to only allow so much and so often. If he's still in pain in between doses, let me know and I'll get him something else.

"Chief, I'm giving you morphine for the pain now. It's going to put you back to sleep but it will help make you feel so much better."

My jaw aches from clenching my teeth and my eyes wouldn't open again even if you used a crowbar, they're squeezed shut so tight.

"Breathe, Judson," Quincy encourages. "In through your nose, out through your mouth. Come on! You can't hold your breath, it only makes it worse." I can't seem to follow her instructions because the pain's so intense. "Breathe, damn it!" Quinn barks at me.

I suck in a deep breath hoping to stop the panic in her voice and at the same time relief rolls through me. Sweet bliss to replace the pain. "I love you, Quinn. I always—" I release the air from my lungs unable to finish my thought and drift off as the darkness overtakes me. Quinn's voice is now a distant memory.

QUINN

I sit cramped up in this chair next to Judson's bed, exhausted, scared and overwhelmed. Seeing a man like him, with the physical strength and determination of an ox, reduced to what lies in that hospital bed makes me want to hurl curse words at God. *Why Judson?* I've asked this question a hundred times since I got here. Once the Colonel realized how upset I was he tried to get me to leave and go to the hotel, but that's not going to happen. Judson saved me all those years ago. Who knows where I'd be now without his intervention. I was a self-destructive mess heading for my own demise when he stepped in, so there's no way in hell I'm leaving his side until I know he's going to be okay. I need to call his mom and Jenny, but it's getting close to time for his next dose of morphine so I'm going to wait until he wakes up and needs it. Judging by his reaction the last time he woke up, he'll be miserable, but this time I won't have to wait to give him relief.

When he told me he loved me the last time he got the dose of morphine I started crying. I was already keyed up because of watching his pain, but the possibility that he loved me was overwhelming. I'm certain it was the drugs talking because he said it as soon as the relief hit and couldn't finish his sentence. I could tell the pain was lessening because all of his muscles relaxed so I shouldn't have cared that he said it, but my hopeful heart couldn't help but grasp on to those words.

As I lean back and rest my head on the back of the chair, I stare at the ceiling, thinking about the night he changed my life. I was 21 years old and I woke up with the cold bathroom floor biting into my back through my thin shirt while vague memories of the night before floated around in my mind. My mouth tasted like someone's shoe after they walked through a cow pasture— that's a side effect of drinking I don't miss at all. I was sore all over, but had no idea why. I did know running into Marcus and Gwen triggered my balls-to-the-wall party mindset that night.

I recall having no idea where I was or whose leg my head was lying on. Not one of my finer moments. Looking up I found a sexy, sleepy, hunk of a man looking down at me. Usually when I woke up with little to no recollection it was with someone I didn't know. However, this time, I did know this guy.

We were both pistol team scholarship students at the university. So we saw each other, often. Judson Rivers was the hottest member of our pistol team. Let me be clear, he was the hottest member of any team, pistol or otherwise, anywhere. We were always friendly, but I never had any indication he was interested in me.

Some things stay with you forever and the tired yet concerned expression on his face is one of those things that even ten years later I can see clear as day. I tried to sit up and move away from him but the room spun so bad I had to plop my head back in his lap. At that point it became obvious the vomit odor in the air was my doing.

"Hurting this morning?" he asked, his voice gravelly from sleep.

"Um...yeah. You could say that," I grumbled, covering my face with my hands, wishing I could hide behind them. This is not the guy you want to have seeing you in this state.

"I knew you would be. You had yourself a really good time, until you didn't anymore." His voice was so deep it rumbled through me, irritating and settling me all at once. Such a peculiar feeling, I remember thinking. The sarcasm would've pissed most people off, but it made the whacked-out situation I was in that morning less horrifying.

"Oh great, a smartass," I mumbled.

A hearty chuckle shook his body and in turn shook my insides. My stomach rolled over again.

"Did we, um...you know?" Averting my eyes, I questioned him, terrified to hear the answer.

He chuckled again. "No, if I'm going to be *um...you know*, it's a requirement that the woman's not actively puking." Mr. Sarcastic struck again and I cringed.

"I was that bad, huh?" *Shit, shit, shit.* Maybe I didn't want the conversation to continue.

"Yeah."

Curiosity got the best of me so I asked, "How long have we been on the floor in here?"

"About five or six hours."

"Why are you still here? You should've left me on this floor and gone home."

"This is my home. You were pretty messed up and I was afraid if I left you on my bathroom floor overnight I'd come in to a corpse in the morning or have to clean up a room full of puke. I wasn't in the mood for either. At least this way I could redirect you to the toilet or call 911 before it was too late."

I groaned in embarrassment. I knew I had to stop this train wreck. Seeing Marcus and Gwen was a trigger, but I should've shown some self-control.

"Quinn. Why didn't you tell me what was going on?"

"Tell you what?" I tried for an unaffected look, but it was hard to hide my expression when he pinned me with an intense stare while my head lay in his lap. Being vulnerable sucked. Not a new feeling for me at the time, but one I hated just the same.

"I don't know what you're talking about, Judson. I had a few too many last night, but look around, this is pretty normal college behavior." My tone was a little snotty, but deflection had become a tried-and-true tactic at that point in my life. You'd think with all the people partying constantly in college no one would even notice me, but I wasn't that lucky.

"I realize we aren't close, but we're teammates and friends. I would've helped you."

I must have been failing miserably at my attempt to appear confused because he continued, "You can act like you don't know what's coming out of my mouth, but you spilled your guts last night in between rounds of puking. We're going to have this conversation or I'm going to the Colonel to let him know how things are going for you on your off time."

He had my attention with that statement. The Colonel, aka retired Colonel Gene Banks, was the coach for our pistol team and the reason I had a partial scholarship. He's also someone I respected and I would've been mortified if he'd found out how I'd been acting. I sat up again and pushed away, but the room took a spin so I found myself hunched over the toilet, dry heaving enough to cause stomach cramps. Sweat had collected on my brow and an overall feeling of exhaustion took over. Judson pulled me back so my butt rested on his thighs and my head was against his chest. I allowed the tears to leak from my eyes as I relaxed against him, but I stayed silent.

"Quincy, I'm not judging you. I'm concerned. You said last night that you slept with that douchebag Marcus Brighton and ended up pregnant, but lost the baby. I have to know the story or I'm going over there to beat his ass just based on this small amount of information. It wouldn't be that big of a deal because that guy is a serious fuckstick, but I'd at least like to have the whole story first."

I still sat there quiet. I couldn't believe I'd told him all of that.

"Quincy, speak up. I'm not kidding; I'm pissed enough to fight." The authoritative tone warned me that he wasn't making idle threats.

I sighed as the lump in my throat grew bigger by the second.

"Yeah, I get that and appreciate you taking care of me and caring enough to want to kick his ass, but there's nothing that can be done. He's a dick. I just can't seem to get myself together and get over it. I'm like a tangled bundle of wires. Not just on the outside, but the inside, too. I almost can't function half the time."

"Brighton isn't worth all of this. You're falling apart at the seams. What else happened? Did he rape you?"

"No, unfortunately I did this to myself."

"Explain. I'm not going to tell anyone. You can trust me, but I need to know the whole truth, Quinn."

I spent the next 20 minutes explaining how I'd had a crush on Marcus since I was a little girl so when he approached me at a party the previous summer I was giddy and ended up hooking up with him. The next morning, I found out that Marcus and Gwen hadn't broken up like he told me the night before, she was just out of the country and he was horny. I could tell the story pissed Judson off, but he looked absolutely murderous when he found out I'd gotten pregnant from the encounter, lost the baby and my ability to ever have kids. Marcus claimed the baby wasn't his so he wouldn't feel any guilt, but I hadn't been with anyone else, so it had to be his. One bad choice and my life was forever changed in a big way.

Judson was quiet for a long time as I lay against his chest lost in thought. He continued to stroke my hair and said, "Well, if I can't go over there and kick his ass then I'm going to stay here and help stop your life from spinning out of control."

I leaned my head back and flipped my eyes to his, holding my breath for several long seconds before asking, "Why? I'm not your responsibility."

"No, you're not, but I care about you and I'm going to help you get through this. It's not going to be easy, but you won't be alone." I remember hoping he wasn't full of crap because I didn't know how much longer I could keep going like I had been. Sighing, my eyes closed as I prayed I wasn't dreaming this conversation. I'd been in need of a lifeline for a long time, but hadn't known how to find one. My close friends would've helped if they knew what to do. Hell, most of them didn't even know what happened to change me. They just knew I'd gone from normal college student to Miss Party Time seemingly overnight. I rested against him again, feeling relieved and so tired I couldn't keep my eyes open.

I woke later that morning to find myself on an unfamiliar bed completely clothed and covered with a navy blue comforter. I rolled to my back to see if anyone was beside me and encountered Judson resting quietly. He was close enough I could have counted his eyelashes if I'd wanted, but he wasn't touching me. A warmth spread through my chest as I realized how respectful and sweet the gesture was. Swinging my legs over the side of the bed, my intent was to sneak out, but he was obviously resting lightly because his eyes popped open and his gruff voice filled the room, "Where do you think you're going?"

"I... I...am going back to my dorm room to get a shower and get ready for class."

"Sit," he commanded.

"I..."

"That wasn't a question. Sit, better yet, lie back down and let's have a little talk. Then I'll drive you back to the dorm." He shocked me enough with his tone of voice that I lay back down. He turned on his side to face me as I faced him. His sleepy blue eyes melted me a little with his evident concern.

His palm wrapped around my jaw and held my face in place so I could look at nothing but his eyes, which burned bright with anger and remorse for me in such a powerful way.

"Quince, I'm sorry for what you've lost, but it's time to come out of this hole. No more bullshit. I'm going to hang by your side until you're strong again. I'm sure Denise means well, but it's impossible to do this stuff alone and she obviously doesn't have a clue how to handle it.

"Marcus is a total douchebag, not worth ruining your life over. I'm sure you wanted kids eventually and I want to rip that fucker limb from limb for taking that away from you, but you can always adopt if you want them when it's time. Right now though it's time to get tough.

"I've got class and a few calls to make to get things lined up for you so I'll be over to pick you up at 4:30 this afternoon. You'd better be there and ready or I won't hesitate to throw you over my shoulder and take you in whatever you're wearing or hunt you down wherever you might be. I'm not kidding."

The whole time he was talking, tear drops trickled down my face, falling off to the pillow steadily. His thumb slid softly under my eyes as he wiped the remaining moisture away.

"I don't know if I can do it. When I drink I don't think about what an idiot I was when I fell for him and gave him the opportunity to take everything from me," I admitted. "If I'd shown some self-control instead of acting like the hormone-crazed college girl I was, I wouldn't be here having this conversation."

"You can do it, Quincy, and I'll help you every step of the way. Time to let go of the past and move on."

"Why? It doesn't make any sense for you to spend your time worrying about me."

"Because you're a good person who was treated badly and left to suffer alone. You don't deserve that. You're my friend and teammate. I want you to know there are still men out there who'll treat you with the respect you deserve. I'm not doing this to get in your pants so don't even go there. Friends only."

I lay there quiet for a while before I said, "Okay."

"Now, let me get up and into my medicine cabinet so I can get you some anti-nausea medicine. I keep it on hand for nights I drink too much. It helps. After you take it I'll drive you to the dorm. I don't care what you do between now and 4:30, but you'd better be showered, teeth brushed and ready to go."

Judson stuck to his word from that day forward. He was by my side every step of the way. Taking me to counseling appointments and AA meetings. He worked out with me and helped me study. During that time, we built a friendship that not only changed my life, but also changed my heart. It taught me how to trust and to love again. He helped give me back the power over my life that an asshole and shitty circumstances took from me. He taught me how to not only survive but to live again. Now I'd like the chance to do the same for him, if he makes it through this.

Chapter Two

JUDSON

Eleven Months Later...

I hate cemeteries. I hate funerals. I hate caskets and I really hate my life right now. I've been back stateside for almost a year and I'm still a fucked-up mess. Every day I feel like I'm drowning and there's no lifeline to grab onto and to make it worse it's going so slowly that I have to watch every second of my downward descent into hell happen with no option of closing my eyes. Depressing, I know.

Right now I'm attempting to climb the hill to the plot where the Colonel will be laid to rest. My leg isn't cooperating on this uneven ground and I'm wishing I would've taken my time with the physical therapist a little more seriously. My arms are as strong as they've ever been but I haven't learned to navigate all terrains with the leg yet and my legs aren't nearly as strong as I'd like.

Ms. Polly, the Colonel's widow, called me last week to tell me he was at the end. I've stayed in touch with them so I knew his health was failing, but I didn't realize it would be this soon. I should've come to see him when she called, but I was too big of a coward. I knew he'd be disappointed and kick my ass for the way I've been living, and I wasn't in the right frame of mind to be respectful to him when he did. I haven't seen him since I was in the hospital in Germany following the explosion, and I barely remember that. The morphine and the extreme pain kept things pretty fuzzy for me.

He's the only person other than my mother and brother that I kept in touch with once I entered the Navy. I sent one letter to Quinn, I promised her one, letting her know that I did in fact survive BUD/S and become a SEAL. The experience was hard as hell, but the training and preparation are what kept me alive, only now I can't quite figure out why I'm still alive. *What did I save myself for?*

I shake those thoughts away as I labor to get up the hill. That's a damn joke in itself. Up until a year ago I was a superior fighting machine, in the best shape of my life and trained for elite tactical maneuvers others could only dream of. Today, I can barely walk myself up a little hill to pay my respects to my mentor and father figure. It's a sad damn day.

As I reach the top, I realize there are a bunch of people here. Men and women in uniform and civilian clothes. Old, young, black, white, Hispanic, you name it they're here. I've never been very outgoing, but after I lost my leg I like being around people even less.

I excuse myself awkwardly maneuvering around people to get to the Colonel's wife where she told me she wanted me. When I finally reach her, she wraps her frail old arms around my middle and holds on tight. Soft sobbing sounds drift up from between us so I rub her back and wait patiently for her to settle down. This is a sweet but tough old woman and I hate to see her hurting like this. She pulls back and looks up at me, patting my cheek affectionately.

"You're sitting with me. You might as well have been our son and I need one right now."

I give her a gentle smile and say, "I wouldn't be anywhere else."

She gestures to the chair next to her so I sit down and pull her tiny hand into mine. Her head rests against my shoulder and the pungent aroma of old lady perfume and aerosol hairspray wafts up into my nose as she settles in.

A chaplain steps up to the podium and clears his throat, drawing our attention and she sits up straight, pulling her hands back to her lap and folding them demurely.

"Ladies and gentlemen, we've come together to pay our respects to Colonel Gene A. Banks. The man is a legend. It seems everywhere I go, someone knows him. He was famous for speaking his mind and telling it like it is. Those who knew him well would also call him an old softie. I wouldn't be able to get away with saying that if he were still here, but he's not, so I will." A light chuckle spreads through the crowd. "He is preceded in death by his sister, Anna Dickerson, and his son, Colin Banks. He's survived by his lovely wife, Polly, of 60 years and his brother, Norton, who was too ill to travel here today. He's also survived by his son, Chief Petty Officer Judson Rivers, and daughter, Officer Quincy Hannigan, who he said may not have been theirs by blood, but are loved by himself and Polly just the same."

The sentiment of that statement hits me with a force I can't explain and tears strain at the back of my eyes. I don't cry, especially when I'm in uniform and never in front of people. However, right now I'm having a hard time controlling my emotions. This whole last year has been an exercise in fighting the onslaught of emotion.

In the same second that I'm bowled over with sorrow I register that the chaplain said, "Officer Quincy Hannigan." I search the crowd, wondering if she's here. I knew she was close to them but didn't realize she was that close. She was with him at the hospital in Germany after I lost my leg, but I never figured out why. In the middle of my own personal hell and only half conscious during that time, I didn't think to ask. I did ask about her in my letters over the years, but never got much of a response from him. A few words here or there to let me know he knew what she was up to, but he never said anything that led me to believe they were this close.

Officer Quincy Hannigan. Officer? Wow, I didn't realize she'd gone into law enforcement. It shouldn't surprise me considering how impressive her marksmanship skills were. I wondered what she was doing after her time with the National Pistol team. If I wasn't so self-consumed, I would've looked her up on the Internet.

The chaplain continues, "Usually, I give the eulogy, but when I met with him last week, the Colonel asked if Officer Hannigan could do it; Of course the answer was yes, who am I to deny a dying man his request?"

My palms sweat, so I wipe them on my pants and hope Ms. Polly doesn't grab my hand again right now. I continue to scan the crowd for Quinn. She's obviously here. My uninjured leg bounces nervously until Ms. Polly rests her hand on it to settle me. Finally, I see the raven-haired beauty step up to the podium and unfold a piece of paper.

She's in a black pencil skirt that hugs her curves perfectly, a white button-down blouse and a black jacket. Her black heels accentuate the muscles in her calves. She's always been athletic, lean and muscular with a hint of womanly curves, time has not changed this fact. I'd love to pull the pins that hold her hair in the elaborate twist-thing at the back of her head and watch as all her silky hair tumbles over her shoulders. The hairstyle makes her appear more adult, more put together than I last remember her, but I always had a thing for the dark, shiny, silky hair she was blessed with. Her eyes lift to the crowd and connect automatically with mine. A small smile plays at her lips before she glances around and begins.

"As you all know by now, I've been close to the Colonel and his wife for many years. He was my coach on the pistol team at Ohio State University, he was my mentor, but he was also a friend and second father to me.

"He scolded me when I did wrong like I was his own child and wiped my tears when I was sad. He cheered me on when I competed and encouraged me to do more, be more and live a full life. The man was a rock, the strongest man I've ever known and I've known some pretty strong men. He was a tough old bird with a soft, beautiful soul and was a man I'll never forget.

"During these last months I was privileged enough to help care for him, and although it pissed him off that he needed caring for, I could tell he still appreciated it. I took the night shift so Ms. Polly could keep a normal schedule, and because he had a hard time sleeping we spent a lot of those hours talking. The man was a wealth of knowledge and experience, but something I took away from those moments was the importance of fighting for who and what you love. Also, making the most out of every moment you have in this life, and the biggest, most life-changing lesson for me, seeing the potential in other people.

"He told me often that sometimes the brightest light shines from the darkest place and I believe he's right about that. Without someone believing that of me at one point in my life I wouldn't be standing here now. I can't say the Colonel *was* loved because the truth is he's *still* loved. I can say with absolute certainty that he will be missed by many.

"The Colonel was highly decorated during his 30-year Air Force career, with three tours in Vietnam, and one in Kuwait. When he retired, he coached the pistol team at the Air Force Academy for 10 years and then at Ohio State University for another 10. In his retirement, he spent a generous amount of time and money on both children's and veterans' charities, while encouraging others to do the same.

"I could go on for hours about the Colonel and all of his

achievements but I know it would just make him mad. He even made me promise to keep this short and sweet. Ms. Polly and I agreed that instead of drawing this out, we'd love for everyone to come by their house following the service, for lunch and to share your own thoughts and memories of the Colonel with us. I'm certain everyone here has something we'd love to hear. He was a good man, an honorable man worthy of the sentiment. May he rest in peace. Thank you all for coming."

She steps away from the podium and back off to the side. The chaplain returns and finishes the funeral, but all I can think about is Quincy and what a gorgeous woman she's grown up to be. She was pretty before, but she's apparently one of those women who grows more stunning as each year passes. I noticed she doesn't have a ring on her finger and she still goes by Hannigan, making me more curious than I should be.

Why isn't a woman as beautiful and well-spoken as she is not tied down? It doesn't make any sense. Now I wish I'd have pushed to get answers from the Colonel over the years. I just assumed she was living back in Ohio near her family and married by now.

As the service concludes, I escort Ms. Polly, awkward limp and all, back to her limo and follow her home. When we arrive at her house I sneak off to the bathroom where I splash some water on my face and take a few minutes to collect myself.

A few pain pills would be helpful right now. Too bad I don't have any with me. I'm sore and don't want to deal with the pain or the mass of people I'll encounter over the next couple of hours. Thoughts like that piss me off because they demonstrate my weakness. I've spent the last 10 years proving I'm anything but weak and had all of that taken away in one split second—a split second I can't change no matter how hard I wish for it.

Once I feel like I'm pulled together, I step out of the bathroom and head down the hallway to a room full of people who must have just arrived. My muscles are stiff, making my limp more pronounced, drawing more attention to my condition and I hate it. I mentally slap myself and work at walking without the gimpy gait.

Ms. Polly is seated on the couch talking with another older woman as I approach and offer to get her a drink. She declines and introduces me. I wish I could tell you her friend's name, but at the same time as the introduction happens I glimpse the black-haired beauty alone on the back porch. Smiling politely, I shake hands with the woman and excuse myself.

As I step out the back door her gaze shifts from the quiet forest behind the house to me, and for a brief second I see a light in her eyes that I've missed for the last 10 years. She gives me a small smile and stands up. I make my way to her, doing my best to stay steady and fluid. Of all the people in this house, it's her I don't want to see my limp. When I'm about two steps away I can't fight the pull of her anymore. I should play it cool and act unaffected, but I know it's just not possible so I move straight in for a hug, praying she doesn't push me away. She doesn't and I breathe a sigh of relief while she rests her head on my chest holding tight around my waist.

I take a deep breath in and let it out slowly, enjoying the sweet scent of her hair, wishing I could carry that smell with me always. God, I've missed her. Without thought I press my lips to the top of her head and let the tears I've been hiding all day fall. It seems like too much is happening and I'm losing ground fast. I never in a million years thought I'd see her again and here we are sharing the same sorrow for the death of a dear friend and almost-father. Life works in the most mysterious ways.

Her lithe, yet curvy body fits perfectly pressed into mine. I've been without the warmth and connection of another human being for so long that it's insanely comforting with her. If she allowed it, I'd stay like this for hours.

Sadly, she pulls away and wipes at her face like she was crying too. Then she takes my hand and tows me to the swing and I wipe the lingering tears on my cheeks away as discreetly as possible.

Once we're seated we both rest in silence for a little bit before she comments, "He really loved you, Judson. He lived for your letters."

I turn to face her, my brow furrowed.

She continues, "It's one of the things he wanted you to have. There are other things too. Ms. Polly will explain when everyone leaves, if she's up for it, but he saved every one of your letters and the last couple of months I spent reading all of them to him again. Nine years of letters is a lot of reading." A smirk crosses her lips, but I can see a tinge of sadness too.

I was sure he read them when I sent them, but I didn't realize they really meant anything beyond a source of information for him. Sometimes writing those letters was the only link I had to the outside world, to people other than my team. I wrote to my mom on occasion, but my correspondence to her was pretty superficial because I didn't want her to worry. I was more open with the Colonel, at least as much as I could be considering the nature of my job. I knew he'd understand with his military history.

"I can't believe he kept them all."

I wish I could remember what I wrote in those letters. I know there were some things I wrote about Quincy but I have no idea what they were now.

"Why didn't you come to see him the last couple of months, Judson?"

I'm quiet. I don't want to answer this and it pisses me off that she put me on the spot, so I don't reply. She groans and stops the swing from moving so she can stand up.

"I'd better go help Ms. Polly. I'm glad you came; it means a lot to her. Keep that in mind when she asks you to stick around. I know it's not your thing, but she needs you, even if it's just for a little while."

Her words hit me like a slap to the face and anger swirls inside me, burning like it has for a long time, churning my gut and pissing me off more. I snatch her hand to halt her as she walks by.

"You have no idea what it's been like for me so don't judge me because I didn't come to see a dying man when he probably wouldn't remember me anyway," I growl through clenched teeth.

My anger is mirrored in her eyes as she responds, "If you don't want to talk about why you were a coward and couldn't face him then don't, but don't you dare act like I'm the jerk here. He loved you like you were his own and you couldn't be bothered. I get it. Poor Judson, life didn't turn out the way you planned. Guess what? It never does. Not for any of us, but I need you to suck it the hell up long enough to help Ms. Polly get through this. Then you can go back to your cave and hibernate if that will make you happy. I'm not trying to be a bitch, but I can't deal with selfish right now, so suck it up." She yanks her arm out of my hold and storms off into the house without another word.

Shit. I didn't mean for things to go that way, but damn. Why'd she have to give me the guilt trip? She has no idea what I've been through. My body still aches, my future's unclear and I'm floating without a damn purpose. That IED took so much from me, she has no idea.

She's right though; I'm a coward. I couldn't let the Colonel see me in the state I'm in, all gimpy and strung out. I still haven't kicked the pills all the way and I'm still an emotional mess. I didn't want to deal with his judgment. If I saw even a little disappointment in his eyes when I faced him, I'm not sure I would've recovered. If I'd shown up during the last couple of months, he'd have seen me for the man I really am: a coward, a loser, and an all-around asshole.

I sit outside stewing in my own piss and vinegar awhile longer, until I finally decide I've had enough. I do my best to move quietly through the house, avoiding people as I go so I won't have to talk, but Ms. Polly catches me in the hall and places a cold wrinkled hand on my cheek. Her watery eyes meet mine before she asks, "I know it's been a long day for all of us, but could you stay for a little bit after everyone leaves? There are some things the Colonel wanted you to have. If it's too much today, we can do it tomorrow. I just know it needs to get done and he hated procrastination so I want to do it soon."

I look into her hopeful eyes and cave. "Yes, Ms. Polly, I can stay after everyone leaves. Can I help to get some things cleaned up right now?"

She pats my cheek. "You're such a good young man. You can clear the trays and take them to Quincy in the kitchen. I think she's started the dishes. Maybe take out the trash. Thank you."

"Yes, ma'am." She shuffles back into the living room to chat some more as I walk around dumping trash and collecting empty cups and trays. When I take them to the kitchen, Quinn doesn't say a word as she continues working.

She's tied her hair up in a messy knot on top of her head and removed her suit jacket. Her sleeves are rolled up her arms and I notice a tattoo in script on the inside of her wrist. I can't read it without getting right up on it, so I leave the kitchen and ponder what could be written there.

A few hours later, everything is cleaned up and Quinn has disappeared in the house somewhere. I'm resting by the fireplace, watching the flames dance as I remember the day I met the Colonel at the shooting range all those years ago.

I was 16 years old and at the range with my dad. He'd taken me there once a week since I was 10 years old to shoot the pistol and the rifle. He always said we had to stay in practice, never knew when we'd need those skills, but my mom told me later that it was my dad's guaranteed time with my brother and me. My brother was an okay shot, but I was a natural. I had a steady hand and almost perfect aim right away.

When I was 15, the owner of the range suggested to my dad that I try a competition, so he signed me up. I did well and enjoyed it, so he signed me up for more. The Colonel was scouting when he saw me at one about a year later and tracked me down. He showed up at the range where I practiced in town and talked to me about attending OSU and being on the team. He stayed in touch until I was ready for college decisions and jock-eyed hard to get me there. Because he was offering me scholarship money for room and board and I wanted out of Colorado Springs, I decided to go. Jenny and my mom wanted me to stay in state, near my hometown, and take over the farm one day, but I wanted different things for my life. Things that would take me much further than a few states away so I compromised by going to college in Ohio. I don't know why I thought I would want to go back home after I got a taste of life outside of Colorado, but I'd convinced myself I just needed a little bit of adventure. So off to Ohio I went.

I'm not sure why, but the Colonel and I started a friend/mentor relationship right out of the gate. At first, I figured it was the way he was with all his shooters, but over time I realized he considered me special and I was further convinced of this when he pulled strings to get me into the Navy immediately and to roll me right into BUD/S after boot camp. No one else slipped right into the Navy or BUD/S that easily. Most had been in the Delayed Entry Program for six months to a year before they even went to boot camp.

Breaking me from the memories, Ms. Polly steps in front of me and hands me a large plastic bin and instructs me to open it. Inside, bundled neatly and tied in yellow ribbon is probably every single letter I've ever written to the Colonel. Quinn said he kept them and they read them, but I thought maybe she was exagger-ating about it being all of them. As I look at the stacks I realize there are probably six or seven hundred letters in here.

My eyes lift to Ms. Polly's and she holds up another box I didn't realize she'd gone and gotten. I close the lid on the box of letters and set it on the floor. Then I put the next box on top and open it up. Ms. Polly sits down next to me as I peek inside. I pull out the first item wrapped in black velvet cloth and realize it's a shadow box of the Colonel's service ribbons. There's a note attached to the outside so I peel it off and open it up.

Dear Judson,

You are the only person left on this earth who would understand what these mean and could learn something from them. As you know, I'm very proud of the time I spent in the Air Force and although I didn't share the worst of my stories with you, I had them. There are some things that happen in times of war that we are unable to share with anyone else due to the horrific circumstances or the fact that the mission was classified. Sadly, it's the nature of the beast.

As you review the ribbons, I want you to know each represents a memory of the time I was in the Air Force, both the good and bad. Over the years I've learned to be proud of every step of my journey because they all brought me back to Polly in the end, and the love of a woman like her is worth every bit of what I went through.

You can throw them away, hide them in a closet or stick them on the wall, but whatever you decide, I hope you'll take a few moments to compare your own ribbons to mine. I think you'll see some similarities you didn't know were there. Be proud of your time in the Navy even if it ended in almost the worst way possible, and I stress "almost" because I've never been more thankful for almost in all my life. When I got the call about your accident and we weren't sure you were going to make it, I swear I was ready to die myself that day. My heart hasn't known that kind of pain since Colin died over 50 years ago. Your life has purpose, you just need to find it again. They say that almost doesn't count unless it's horseshoes and hand grenades; well they forgot to say IEDs too. For us that's the truth.

More than anything I want you to know I'm proud of you and I believe in you. You will find your place and make a difference, I'm certain of it.

Sincerely,
Colonel Gene A. Banks

The next thing I find in the box is a photo album, so I open it up and on the first page is a group photo of our pistol team at OSU my first year there. The next couple of pages are all the clippings from the papers and trade magazines for my accomplishments while I was at OSU. Following that he has all four years of Quincy's time there. According to this, she was selected to train with the national team here in Colorado Springs after her senior year and she accepted. Past that, my picture from the Navy is in there and every picture I sent him is tucked neatly within the plastic coating.

Following that are pictures of Quincy over the last 10 years with different hairstyles and different clothes. A few newspaper articles since she started at Denver PD and then the last few pages are blank like he meant to put more in there but just hadn't made it that far.

I look up to find Ms. Polly watching me.

"When I asked him if he wanted me to separate the pages and give yours to you and hers to her, he said no. He said you missed out on knowing what went on in Quincy's life while she knew what was going on in yours. He wanted me to share this with you. He thought you'd want it. If you don't, I can remove her pages and give them to her."

I shake my head. "He was right. I do want to see this. How did she know about me? How did she see all of this?"

"Over the years she's spent a lot of time with us and made no secret of her curiosity about your life and career so Gene shared with her. He always suspected she was in love with you, but never really gave her any grief about it. When the call came in that you were injured, she was staying with Gene for a few days and I was at my sister's house in California so she accompanied him to the hospital in Germany to be with you.

"I'm sure you don't remember any of that. They both said you were out of it, but Gene said she was a mess. Anyway, that's her story to tell if you care to ask her. He just thought you'd want to see it. The last thing in there is a little tape recorder and a tape with a message he recorded for you to listen to when you have time. I have no idea what's on it since he wouldn't let us anywhere near his room when he made it. Quincy tried to explain that there are more modern ways to do that but he was a stubborn old goat when it came to technology. He wanted to do it this way so forgive him for using archaic technology."

After I thank her I collect the boxes and carry them to my truck. Then I step back inside to say goodnight and hug Ms. Polly. I know Quincy's pissed at me so I should probably stay away and give her space, but something is pushing me to say goodbye to her. I wander back to the kitchen only to find it empty. Ms. Polly enters behind me so I ask, "Where might I find Quincy?"

"Try her room. Down the hall, last door on the right."

As my heart beats heavily in my chest I knock on her door.

She calls out, "Come in!"

I turn the knob and step inside. Relaxed on the love seat by the bay window, she lifts her eyes to mine. Her legs are curled up under her, hair still up, book in hand and she's now wearing a pair of sexy black-framed librarian glasses. I feel a stirring in my pants and the shock of it must register on my face because her forehead wrinkles as she asks, "Are you okay?"

I'd love to tell her I'm great, but I don't think she'd be quite as impressed by the beginnings of a hard-on as I am. This is the first time I've had any kind of action down there since the accident. The doctor told me not to worry about it, the function would eventually return, it's mental more than physical, but I was afraid it never would. For a guy my age, no blood flow to the dick is a terrifying thought.

I cross my hands down low, trying to discreetly cover up. She'd never understand. Who gets a boner the same day he buries someone close to him?

"Yeah, I'm okay. I just wanted to come and say goodbye."

She lifts the glasses from her face and sets them on top of the book she's placed on the table next to where she's seated. When she stands and takes a few steps toward me I realize my heart is pounding harder than it was when I knocked on the door, like I've run a few miles. It's been far too long since I've had this kind of reaction to a woman.

"How long are you staying?" I inquire.

"A couple of weeks. I promised the Colonel I'd help Ms. Polly take care of everything. We have to go through some things out in the shed this week too. Are you leaving to go back East right away?"

"No. I'm moving back here. I'm staying at one of those extended stay hotels by the interstate until I can find something. If you need help going through any of his stuff or lifting some of those things, let me know. I don't have a lot on my schedule yet."

Her head tilts and her eyes narrow like she's trying to figure out if my offer is genuine.

I lift up my hands in a gesture of surrender as I say, "I'm not saying you can't do it, just that I'm available if you want help. I'll write my cell number down and you can use it, or not."

She watches me intently as I jot down my number and leave it on the table. Then I walk back over, place my hands on her shoulders, kiss her forehead, lingering a little longer than I should so I can absorb the scent of her again, and limp out the door. I don't wait to see if she has anything to say or any reaction to the chaste kiss. My heart and body both ache and I wish I were a different man. A better man. One that could have a woman as beautiful and amazing as she is and be worthy of her.

There are a million things I want to say to her, but can't. Ten years and 100 regrets later, I find that the man I am now is a coward who can't express a single emotion or tell the truth to the one woman he still loves. She never knew I fell in love with her all those years ago. I was too busy escaping reality and following a selfish dream in the Navy to tell her the truth about my feelings. I wanted her to have a better life than one of waiting on her husband to come back from whatever godforsaken corner of hell the Navy sent me to. I kept quiet and left her standing in front of her dorm and didn't see her again until Germany. By then I was in no shape to have a heart-to-heart. I barely remember anything beyond confusion and pain from that two-week period. She's right, I'm still a coward 11 years later.

I hug Ms. Polly and tell her I'll see her soon. She already has my number so I encourage her to call me if she needs me. I pull away from their amazing house on top of the hill with Ms. Polly in my rearview mirror waving as I go.

When I arrive at my hotel I lug the bins inside, grab a beer from the fridge and press Play on the cassette. Did he realize how much it would mean to me to be able to listen to his voice? I wish I knew. For the first few years after my dad died I always wished I could hear his voice and of course I didn't have a recording of it anywhere.

Two beers and a half hour later I'm untying the bow around the first batch of letters, ready to read them as he's instructed. I have no idea why he's pushing so hard for me to read them. I wrote them, I should know what was said. I'm the one who said it in the first place, but he swears there's something to learn from this exercise so I'm starting it.

After the first 10 letters, I realize a few things. One, I wasn't quite as worldly as I thought I was at 21 years old. Two, I was madly in love with Quincy and not as subtle about it as I thought I was. I wonder if I were to ask the guys from my team if they'd say they knew it too. I was never a big talker or bullshitter, but after joining the Navy I got quieter, even less in your face than before. I'm not sure if that was a survival tactic or I just didn't have much to say. I'm surprised by how loquacious I was in the letters. I don't remember that being the case.

I entered the Navy at one of the lowest points in my life. If I would've had to wait to go to boot camp like all other American recruits, I'm not sure I would've done it with some time and perspective on my side. After I expressed what I wanted in the weeks following my dad's death, the Colonel called in a favor or two and with my ASVAB scores, doors were quickly opened and I was shoved through. It was up to me to prove I belonged there.

BUD/S was physically the hardest thing I'd ever done in my life at that point, but it still came easier to me than it did to most of the other guys. The Colonel had a theory that I'd become emotionally detached after the death of my father, making it easier to navigate the more mentally torturous training we went through. He probably wasn't far off the mark. The hardest part for most of the guys wasn't the physical torture we endured, it was the mental stress.

While reading these letters, I find it funny how I'm able to see from a different perspective how often I asked about or mentioned Quinn. In my head it was only occasionally, but so far, all 10 letters ask about her in great detail. He was always good to answer me back but he kept things vague. There are so many things I want to know now that I realize he never answered them for me. Why isn't she married? Is she seeing anyone? Where will she live when she leaves Ms. Polly's house? Is she on a leave of absence from work or did she quit? I probably have twenty more questions, but the biggest question of all is, How do I walk away again now that I can see what I've been missing? It's too bad asking her straight out doesn't seem to be an option.

Two days later, I'm sitting at my mom's apartment drinking coffee with her when I receive a text from Quinn asking if I can help them in the garage later in the day. The smile that hits my face at her request draws instant suspicion with my mother.

"What's got you all smiley? I haven't seen you look that pleased in a long time."

"It's Quincy, a friend of mine from OSU. She's helping Ms. Polly take care of everything at the house. They need help with boxes in the garage so I'll be going over there later."

I'm not expecting the grin that spreads across her face. "I know who she is. When you were in the hospital in Germany she called me every day. She knew I couldn't get there so she kept me updated. The Colonel was having a hard time and needed her help. Any interest?"

My eyes flick to hers and narrow. "No, Mom. She's pretty put together. She wouldn't have anything to do with a guy like me. Besides, I have nothing to offer a woman anymore."

My mom knows I haven't dated seriously since I went into the Navy, not since Jenny. One-night stands were the closest I got to women.

Jenny was my high school sweetheart and although I loved her, I already knew once I was away at college that something had changed between us. I now realize that when my dad died I was able to use that as an excuse to break things off with her. She'd been patiently waiting in our hometown so we could start our life together, but I no longer wanted that. I wanted to serve my country and see the world and have more of an adventure than college in Ohio. I wasn't ready to work a nine-to-five job and start a family at that point. His death allowed me to do that with good reason. It also relieved me of a lot of guilt when it came to ending things with Jenny.

I thought my mom was upset with me about the breakup, but it turns out she understood. She said she felt like my dad settled for her and stayed in our town because it was what she wanted. She said she always wondered if he regretted it and she didn't wish that on anyone. She said that one day, Jenny would've realized asking me to stay was selfish and would have been sorry. She was pleased I was strong enough at the time to walk away and live my dream.

My mother loved my father with a burning passion and I suspected my dad felt the same. Although Mom told me, as the years moved on she began to understand what she took from him, and when he died she mourned the loss of those experiences for him.

"Honey, you still have plenty to offer a woman. You need to start believing that again. Losing half of your leg hasn't lessened your worth as a man."

I don't reply because I don't want to tell her I don't think I can perform like a man should or that I've had issues with prescription medications and alcohol and am very unstable. Or that I feel a lot of guilt that I'm not going to be able to get rid of for being the only one who got to come home. Nope, I just let her statement go without comment.

One of the first few days I was home and ran into Jenny and

two of her three children at the supermarket. It was the first time I'd seen her since right after my father's death. She looked exactly the same except with a little more weight on her, which I'm assuming is leftover baby weight. That didn't detract from her beauty in the least though. Other than one child running laps around her legs and the other drooling everywhere, it was obvious she was living her dream. We didn't say much. We exchanged pleasantries briefly and then said goodbye, but it was good to see her happy.

I was always worried I'd see her out in town and regret my choice or it would upset her, but seeing her like that only reinforced the notion that I made the correct decision when I ended things.

She married a guy who graduated a year ahead of us in school, about two years after I left for the Navy. He's the local car and property insurance salesman in town. They started their family a year later and moved into a huge house in a prominent neighborhood. I heard she's the president of the PTA and is in charge of the Presbyterian church's bake sale every year. She's living the life she wanted.

I text a response to Quinn, noting I'll be there about three this afternoon if that's okay, and go back to dodging my mom's probing questions.

QUINN

I'd love to slap Judson's arrogant, beautiful face. When I looked up at the funeral and saw him sitting next to Ms. Polly I couldn't help the smile that appeared. I'm so pissed at my traitorous mind for allowing the lapse in judgment. If I could've made a choice with my reaction, I would've scowled at him. I'm still really pissed that he didn't see the Colonel before he died.

He does look amazing though. Dress blues never looked better on any man, anywhere. They seem to make his already broad shoulders wider, more intimidating. His cleanly shaven face, more handsome with age, forced my heart to beat faster the same way it did all those years ago. Although his eyes were weary, there was still a depth there I wanted to get lost in.

After the funeral, when I asked him about not visiting the Colonel, I was so pissed my head could have blown off of my shoulders. I tried to rein it in. In fact, I promised myself I wouldn't even ask, but when he approached me I knew I had to. The Colonel loved and adored Judson like he was his own son. He lived for the letters and I knew a visit from him at the end would have meant the world.

The last few months of taking care of the Colonel and helping Ms. Polly have been really difficult, but they were filled with love, laughter and wisdom. I'd never change the decisions I made to help. It's been worth every minute. I just have to decide what I want to do next.

I'm not sure I want to continue down the same path I've been on at the Denver Police Department. Being a female police officer is not as difficult as it once was, but there are still a lot of older men on the force who believe a woman's place is in the home, not working, and especially not on the streets with a badge. Those particular men made my job more difficult every chance they got. I could have reported a couple of them for sexual harassment, but I wasn't about to stoop to their level. I knew they were trying to get a reaction out of me. Trying to piss me off enough so I'd quit. I held my own but it wore on me after a while.

My phone buzzes on the nightstand across the room so I grab it. It's Jeff. Crap, I thought he agreed to give me space. We've been dating for two years. I thought things were going just fine until he dropped the marriage bomb on me. I, of course, freaked out. That's not happening. I have no interest in being tied down. I can't have kids so what's the point? Not that I'd cheat on him. In fact, I didn't date much before him. I just don't see the point.

Marriage is for people who want a family. I can't have one so I don't see the need.

I told Jeff I needed time to think and space to do it when I left Denver. He was pissed I took a leave of absence to take care of the Colonel. He told me I was screwing up my career by doing it. He's never understood the relationship I had with the Colonel and Ms. Polly, but I don't give a damn. After the last conversation, I told him I needed him to back off until I could decide what I wanted. I texted to let him know when the Colonel died and to let him know I haven't decided what I want. He hasn't responded, until now. I was almost afraid he'd show for the funeral.

I slide my finger across the screen to reveal the text:

Jeff: U doing okay?

Me: Good as can be expected. Everyone just left the house.

Jeff: Can I c u this week?

Me: I don't think that's a good idea. I'm helping Ms. Polly tie up all the loose ends like I promised. I'll call u in a few days.

Jeff: I want 2 c u. I miss u.

Me: I'm sorry. I'm just dealing with a lot and trying 2 keep everything under control.

Jeff: How much longer do I need to wait? Either u want me or u don't.

Me: It's not that easy.

Jeff: It's not as hard as you're making it. Plenty of women would jump at the chance 2 marry me.

Me: You know my issues but if u want 1 of the plenty then feel free to go there. My stance on marriage is never going to change.

Jeff: That's not what I meant & u know it.

Me: It sounded like a threat to me.

Jeff: I don't want 2 fight. I just want 2 c u.

Me: Give me a week and I'll come 2 Denver.

Jeff: OK, I love you, Quinn.

I don't respond. Instead I turn off my phone and go back to reading my book. I'm not sure that I love him anymore or that I ever did, which is a big issue right now. I don't want to hurt him. I'm a mess and I'm certain half of it has to do with seeing Judson again, the one man I'm certain I've loved.

I'm sure Marissa from records is happy as hell that I took the leave of absence. That woman has been shamelessly flirting with Jeff for years. I'm sure she threw a party when I left. Hell, for all I know he's hooked up with her since I've been gone. In fact, I'd be willing to wager money he has. Jeff's not the kind of guy to deny himself what he wants and his libido is higher than most so I'm certain he's feeding his appetite. The sad part about it is I'm not even mad. In fact, I'm not feeling anything about that possibility at all. Shouldn't I be upset about the man I supposedly love hooking up with other women?

This morning Ms. Polly made me text Judd, insisting we need his help. His response was not what I expected. I thought he'd make up an excuse about why he couldn't. I was surprised by the quick yes I received. I'm having a hard time believing that he'll be here for any of this when he had such a tough time making it before the Colonel died.

The rumble of his truck and the bang of his door closing reach my ears before I see him. Ms. Polly is still in the house and I'm in the garage surveying the situation, deciding where to start.

When I turn to greet him, I'm halted in my tracks while visions of a naked college-age Judson assault my memory on rapid replay. My breath hitches and I curse myself for the moment of weakness. The clothes he's wearing are similar to what he wore when we were in college. Yesterday, he was in his dress blues and looked like the thirty-one-year-old man he should be. Today he looks like he stepped out of a scene from my memory, and when it comes to him there are some really good memories to choose from. If there wasn't a hardness lingering behind his eyes, which wasn't there all those years ago, I'd swear we'd gone back in time.

Shit, it's going to be a long afternoon. I hate having this reaction after all these years. It's not like he showed up here in a tux or anything. His broad, ripped shoulders have his old T-shirt pulled tight across his chest and the perfectly worn-out, light-colored blue jeans look so soft from age I want to touch them to find out for sure. They seem to hang perfectly off his narrow hips. Damn that's hot, even with the little bit of extra weight he's carrying in his midsection from lack of cardio exercise. Reflexively, I lick my lips and will myself to make eye contact with him. When I do I'm met with his signature smirk that tells me he knows exactly what I was thinking about. I do my best to wipe my expression clean. It's been years since I've seen that smirk, but it still has the same panty-melting effect on me.

"Hey, thanks for coming," I comment, aiming for nonchalant.

His blue eyes twinkle when he answers, "My pleasure. Are you ready to get started?"

"As soon as Ms. Polly comes back. Whatever we don't take, she wants us to gather for donation to AMVETS. They're bringing a truck out tomorrow to tote all of this away."

He nods thoughtfully and turns to scan the room.

"Does she want to keep anything in here?" he asks.

"Only a small bag of tools to take to her new place. There isn't room for anything else. She seriously wants us to take whatever we want. I called dibs on the lawn mower; mine took a crap in the fall and I've dreaded buying a new one. His is five years old and is in better condition than my car. I plan to buy a little house soon and will need it. Why don't you have a look around and see what he's got in here."

"It feels weird going through someone else's stuff, doesn't it?" he asks, chewing on the side of his lip.

"Yeah, but it's also kind of cool. It's like getting a sneak peek into a private section of his mind. He was even more methodical than I suspected."

Judd strolls to the back wall where all of the woodworking

tools are neatly lined up and runs his fingers over them while a thoughtful expression plays on his handsome face.

"The Colonel spent hours teaching me how to use this stuff when we were in Columbus. While most people were out partying, I was doing this kind of stuff with him. We made these amazing nightstands out of cherrywood that I wish I would have taken from him when he offered back in the day."

"He still has them," I mention.

"He does? I didn't see them."

"They're in his room. He was really proud of those. He must have told me how you guys made those together about 10 different times. He made Ms. Polly promise that she'd will them to you when she dies."

I look up to find his eyes glassy with the knowledge I shared. He turns away abruptly and busies himself with thumbing through some papers on the workbench.

"So what made you decide to move back here?" I probe, as curiosity gets the best of me.

"I had nowhere else to go. I have no idea what my next step is and my mom has been asking me to come back for a couple of months. I'm finally at the point where I can do my physical therapy anywhere, so I just decided to do it." He shrugs and continues what he's doing. I take a moment, while he's turned around, to admire the thick thighs and muscled butt his jeans hug with perfection. His T-shirt is worn a little thin, so the collar is stretched a bit and the exposed skin between the collar and his earlobe beckon me to lick a long, slow line until I reach the spot that's really sensitive for him right behind his ear. His voice snaps me out of the naughty daydream I'm brewing in my mind and I flush, embarrassed at my thoughts. One minute I'm mad at him and the next I'm molesting him with my thoughts. *What is wrong with me?*

"Why did you move in with the Colonel?"

"They needed help and he refused to let a stranger in his home at night. I guess his old-school paranoia never went away. He asked me when I was visiting after he was diagnosed. I thought about it for a few days and decided to do it. I took a leave of absence from work, packed up most of my stuff and moved in here."

"Where were you living at the time?"

"A little house I was renting in Denver. It's a cool town, but I had been considering leaving the force for a while anyways so I decided to give up the house. If I move back, I want to buy a little house similar to the one I was living in.

"I've been looking at other career options and have even been looking at a few houses. If I don't go back to Denver, I'll probably stay in the area as long as Ms. Polly is living and then maybe go back to Cincinnati later on. My family is a little pissed I never moved back there after my time with the national team. I just wasn't ready I guess. What's your plan now?"

Ms. Polly steps back into the garage before he can answer and says, "Oh good, you found his woodworking tools, Judson. You're going to take it all, right? Gene was really hoping you would. He always said you were a natural with it."

"I can't take all of this Ms. Polly. It's too much, besides I don't even have a house yet."

"It's not too much for a father to give a son, not even close, and that's what you were to him. I can hold it until you get a place. Now that that's settled, let's get the rest of this junk figured out."

I laugh out loud because that's just the way she is. Most women in her situation would probably still be dressed in black while crying their mourning tears, but not Ms. Polly. She has things she wants to take care of, so no one will see her in anything less than warrior-woman mode. It's how she survived the Colonel's time in Vietnam and Kuwait and part of what he adored about her. The woman is a rock. I know she misses him but she also wants to get things done.

Throughout the day I sneak peeks at Judson's ass as it flexes in those jeans, or admire the way his back muscles contract under the thin cotton of his T-shirt. It's torture to look and not be able to touch. Ms. Polly catches me once and lets out a little giggle and my eyes bug out at being caught. Judson seems oblivious the whole time, thank goodness. Although I can't lie and say it doesn't bother me a little that he's not affected by me in the slightest. I guess a guy who looks like him and is a Navy SEAL probably has a bunch of 20-year-old beauty queens laid out for him on a regular basis. A 32-year-old spinster with a few grey hairs isn't going to get noticed. Besides, I'm still a little mad at him anyway. I sigh out loud and continue working.

By dinnertime we're all tired. His limp is more pronounced and Ms. Polly's eyes are sagging. We eat the pizza she ordered and Judson says his goodbyes, letting us know he'll be back tomorrow to oversee the AMVETS donation for us because I'm taking Ms. Polly to the Social Security office and to see her lawyer.

* * *

I've been lying in bed for two hours trying to go to sleep but not finding much luck in that department. Thoughts of Judson keep rolling through my head. My brain is having a hard time understanding that Judson, the man who cared so deeply for those around him and made love to me 10 years ago is long gone, replaced by one who doesn't really care about much and definitely not about me. Can time change a man that much? Sure, feelings can fade but basic caring? It doesn't match with the man I knew or the one from the Colonel's letters. The man who wrote those letters is not the man I've seen.

I flip the light back on and pull out my romance novel, hoping to have something else to concentrate on for a little while. I'm about three pages into it when my cell phone rings. Who the heck would be calling me this late? Usually it's Denise, my childhood best friend, when it's at an odd hour, but she has an undercover case she's working right now so I know it's not her. The caller ID indicates that it's a Colorado Springs number.

"Hello?"

"Um... Do you know a dude by the name of Judson Rivers?" a gruff, unfamiliar voice asks.

I sit up, suddenly worried that something has happened to him. "Yeah, I know Judson. Why?"

"I need you to come pick him up or I'm calling the cops and he's a vet so I hate to do that."

"What do you mean?"

"Lady, he's drunk as a damn skunk and passed out on my bar face-first. He's been going on and on about you all night so I figured I'd try you before I call the cops."

"How'd you get my number?"

"He left his cell phone sitting on the bar with no lock screen. I just typed in Quincy and this was the only name that popped up. Now are you gonna come get him or should I just call the police?"

I huff out a frustrated breath and reply, "Give me your address and I'll pick him up."

He rattles off the address and I realize it's a bar not far from the interstate, which I'm sure means it's close to his hotel.

I climb out of bed, yank my hair into a ponytail, and pull on a pair of jeans, a sweatshirt and flip-flops. I'll probably freeze my toes off, but I don't want to dig around for matching socks right now. Then I leave a note for Ms. Polly and head towards The Golden Leprechaun, where I'm told Judson has taken up residence I don't know how he has the energy to be out drinking, after all the work we did today. My body is exhausted. I also wonder why he's drinking; I thought the Colonel said he was clean and sober.

As I walk through the doors I realize quite quickly this place is a dump. The clientele is shady and all of the scuzzy men without a bleach-blond bimbo glued to them clocked me the second I rolled through the door. It doesn't even matter that I look like I did when I was up all night studying for finals, it only seems to matter that I'm fresh female meat. *Great.*

I can drop an asshole in one move if I need to, I'd just prefer to keep things civil tonight. I squeeze through the crowd and allow my eyes to roam the length of the bar, still not seeing Judson. A shrill whistle draws my attention to the other end of the room where a burly, bearded man is drilling holes into me with his eyes. In front of him is Judson, face down on the bar exactly as the guy described. His hand is still wrapped around an empty shot glass. He's wearing a long-sleeved Henley so I at least know he's been back to the hotel to shower since I saw him this afternoon.

"Hey, I'm Quincy," I comment to the barkeep.

"Yeah, I figured. We don't get many classy women in this joint so I knew it had to be you."

"How long has he been here?"

"Couple of hours, but he was hittin' the booze pretty heavy. As big as he is I thought he could hold his liquor a little better, but I guess not. He's been in here off and on several days over the past week and I've sent him home in a cab two of those times, so I know he likes to tie them on, but he seemed particularly wound up tonight. I'm not sure what kind of issues you two have, but he didn't want to let it go. Give the boy another chance, he obviously cares and he sure don't belong in a place like this."

I look at him skeptically. "Isn't this your bar?"

He shakes his head, "Nah, it's my brother's and it's an okay place, but a man like him shouldn't be here every night drowning in the juice. He should be warming the bed of a woman like you."

"Okay, thanks. Can you help me get him to my car? There's no way I can lift him if he won't walk."

He places two fingers between his lips and gives another ear-piercing whistle. Everyone stops what they're doing to look over at us. The bartender catches the attention of two large, hairy bikers and asks, "Frank, can you and Joey help carry the big guy to her car?"

The two frightening men lumber over and slide under his armpits, then easily drag/carry him to my car. Once they've gotten him inside I pass them a 20-dollar bill and thank them for their time. My question now is, how am I going to get him inside the hotel? After a few minutes of contemplation, I give up.

I'm not going to even try. One of us would end up getting hurt so I drive him to Ms. Polly's and pull into the garage. I run into the house and grab a couple of blankets, my fuzzy slippers and a bucket just in case he decides to puke. I cover him up and lean his seat back. Then I do the same for myself, shifting the best I can to my side so I can keep an eye on him. After about a half hour, light snoring sounds drift from his parted lips and instead of being annoyed I find it cute. He reminds me of a little boy. The skin on his face no longer has lines or grooves as he reclines, totally relaxed. His full lips and five o'clock shadow call to my fingers, begging me to touch him. I fight the urge, afraid if I start, I won't stop and that's just creepy since he's sleeping. It takes me at least another 20 minutes before I doze off.

I wake a couple of hours later when warm fingers trail across my cool cheek. My eyes flutter open to find Judd watching me closely. "Where are we?" he asks in a whisper.

"Ms. Polly's garage."

"Why?"

"Because you were passed out drunk and I'm not strong enough to haul you inside your hotel."

"How did you know I was drunk?"

"The bartender called me, said you'd talked about me all night so he looked for my name in your phone and wanted me to come get you or he'd call the cops. I decided I didn't want to bail you out of jail so I just picked you up."

"You should have left my dumb ass in the car."

"Nah, I wouldn't leave you out here alone. I was ready to hold your hair should you need it. I do believe I owe you that." I lift the bucket and smile at him.

He groans. "I'm sorry. I... I... I..."

"It's okay. I recall you had it much worse when you took care of me. I just had to sleep in a car. You okay? I'm a little worried. The bartender said you've been there several nights in the last week. I thought you weren't drinking anymore."

He tilts his head away so our eyes are no longer locked and answers, "I'm fine. It's been a rough week, nothing more. Nothing you can do, Quinn. It's just life."

"I'm not trying to be your savior, just your friend."

"Yesterday you didn't even want to be that. Why the sudden change?"

"That was never the case and you know it. I was only pissed that you didn't make the effort to see the Colonel when you knew what it would mean to him. I care about you, Judson. I have for years, so lose the attitude and talk to me."

"I have nothing to say. It's just life, which is nothing like I expected it to be."

"Yeah, well most of us can say the same thing."

"Whatever, Quinn. Your life could be whatever you want it to be, there's nothing holding you back."

"I'm not going to sit here and play the poor-me game with you, Judson. Bottom line is, I give a shit about you. I have since college. I didn't stop caring because you stopped caring for me. I lived for every bit of information I could scrape out of the Colonel about you over the years. I dropped everything like a damn hot potato when you were hurt, not because I had to, but because I couldn't be anywhere but where you were. I needed to know you were going to be okay. Now you can keep acting like a self-involved asshole or you can give me your hand and let me help you up. It's your choice, but I won't beg you."

You can cut the tension in the air with a knife, it's so thick.

He says nothing so I open the garage door with the press of a button and back out. I drive toward the interstate and ask, "Which hotel?"

He gives me a quick one-word answer like even that's too much for him. I'm so pissed at him right now I could slap him upside his stubborn head, and I'm equally pissed at myself for letting him get to me. I should know better than to think he could care even a little for me when he was able to walk away all those years ago and send no more than one letter over all that time. Hoping for anything else is stupid.

I pull up to the front entrance of the hotel. He gets out without even a thank you, shuts the door and hobbles inside, pissing me off further. I smack my hands on the steering wheel in frustration and give a little scream. Once I realize I'm acting like an idiot I drive back to Ms. Polly's and go straight to bed.

Chapter Four

QUINN

WARM HANDS TRAVEL SLOWLY up the outside of my thighs and I squirm in anticipation. It's been so long since I've been touched so reverently. Calloused fingers brush the edges of my hip bones and tug my panties gently down my legs. He hooks his hands behind my knees and spreads me wide. Warm breath flows over the lips of my sex and I whimper, hoping for relief soon. A wet swipe of a tongue parts the sensitive flesh and my back arches off the bed as I beg to be taken. I want to see his expression as he tastes me, but it's pitch-black.

"Please let me see you. I want to watch," I plead, but I know it won't change a thing. We continue on in the dark.

Forcing myself to relax again, I allow my legs to drop open more and his appreciative growl reverberates against me. Another swipe with that teasing tongue and I demand, "Again! More!"

"Always so greedy. The answer is no. I'm in charge, now lie back and relax and if you're a good girl I might let you watch me."

I moan at the vision I conjure in my head. His fingers spread me farther as he begins a steady twirl of his tongue and my hips push against his forearms, which are effectively holding me down. It feels like this goes on forever and I'm on the cusp of release when he sucks my clit into his mouth and flicks quickly with his tongue. The world spins and stars explode in a brilliant light show behind my eyelids. I shoot straight up in bed, crying out, only to realize it's a dream. I'm panting, almost breathless and so turned on. It's not unusual for me to have these dreams that Judson stars in, it's been a while since it felt so real though.

Seeing him must have triggered this one. I pad into the bathroom and splash some water on my face, hoping to cool my libido down a bit. I take a gulp of water and crawl back in between my sheets, praying I'll be able to fall back asleep after that.

* * *

We pull into the driveway after running all of Ms. Polly's errands to find the AMVETS truck still in the driveway. Judson is standing with his arms crossed talking to a man with a clipboard. The man shakes his hand, grabs one last box, closes the rear door, climbs in the truck and pulls away.

Ms. Polly gives Judson a hug and thanks him for helping. I go straight to the front door without a word. After dealing with Mr. Asshole last night I'm not in the mood for his shit, even if Ms. Polly thinks I'm being rude.

I go to my room and curl up on the couch with the book I've been reading for a few days and wait for him to leave.

Thirty minutes later Ms. Polly comes into the room and sits on the love seat next to me. She drops her head to the back of the couch, looks at the ceiling and says, "Gene was a real asshole before he figured out he loved me."

My mouth drops open. I've never heard her cuss before.

"I'm not blind, honey. The two of you have been in love for years. I just wish you'd do something about it. I'm thinking it will have to be you who makes the move though. He may not be strong enough to do it on his own. He is a man after all."

I haven't said a word, still in shock. Her head rolls on the back of the couch so she can look at me.

"I'm old, not dead. Gene read me each and every letter Judson wrote and some you wrote too. We talked extensively about it. We both feel you two are meant to be together. Why are you fighting it? Is it because of Jeff?" She doesn't wait for me to answer before she continues, "Let me explain something to you. Jeff is not the man for you. If he was, you never would've left Denver when he brought up marriage. And he would've been here to visit while Gene was sick. Don't get me started on the fact that he wouldn't have left you to sit alone at a funeral."

"He didn't come to visit or to the funeral because I told him not to. He asked, but I didn't want to have the discussion about marriage during all of this and if he were here in person he would bring it up. As for Judson, I think you're mistaken. He doesn't feel anything for me. We were friends for a while before he went into the Navy. He saved me and I loved him for it. And then...I just loved him. I mean, really loved him.

"I wanted to beg him to stay, but knew I had to let him go. We had one night before he left and I swear it was the best night of my life, but it didn't mean enough to him for him to stay. I prayed every day for 10 years that I'd get more than the one letter, but I never did. I accepted the fact that he doesn't feel the same about me a long time ago."

She opens her mouth to interject and I stop her by holding her hand and continuing what I have to say. "When he came back for the funeral I was still pissed at him for not making the effort to say goodbye to the Colonel so I gave him some lip. He got mad and gave it back. We've been snippy with each other that way. Then last night I got a call from a bartender saying he was drunk and kept talking about me and I needed to come get him so they didn't have to call the cops on him. I got out of bed and picked him up.

"I stayed with him to make sure he was okay. He woke up and

before the conversation was over he was a jerk again. It's been too many years of hoping for a response from a man who doesn't feel anything for me and I'm tired of being disappointed. As for Jeff, I don't want to marry him. I plan to break things off completely."

"I understand. I won't tell you all the ways Gene was a jerk to me and how bad things got after Colin died, but I will tell you that I learned when you love a man like him you have to be prepared to fight. Those kind of men have the souls of warriors and tend to fight everything in life, not just for the things they want, but also at times against them.

"I've known Judson since he was a junior in high school, so I know him better than he thinks. He's fighting for his life right now. That bomb took more than his leg. It took his direction and his confidence, it took the future he expected and the family he'd made amongst those men. He's no longer part of them and no longer part of civilian life.

"He needs you to help him find his way just as he helped you all those years ago. Now," she pats my leg and instructs, "quit feeling sorry for yourself and pissed at him. Go fight for him. Show him he's worth it even without the leg. If I were 50 years younger, I'd certainly be trying to show him something." She gives me a playful wink, pats my leg again and stands. Right before she walks through the door to leave she advises, "Call Jeff and tell him the truth. You don't love him and won't marry him. If your first instinct isn't to say yes a hundred different ways, he needs to find someone else." She taps the doorframe twice to punctuate her point and strolls back out of the room.

Did that really just happen? Could what she's saying be true or is Judson being an asshole and she doesn't want to see it? Could he really feel that lost and out of place? I never thought of that. I can't imagine Judson, with his steady strength, having the problems she's talking about even after the physical trauma he's been through.

I pick up my phone to call Jeff.

"Hello?"

"Hey, we need to talk," I say.

"Okay," his voice is hesitant. "Go ahead."

"I don't want to get married. I know that's what you want. I won't ever want that. I can't have kids and I see no reason to do it. I think it's time we split up for good. I care about you and I want you to have all the things in life you want, but I won't be the person to give them to you."

A frustrated sigh fills the quiet before he says, "Why are you doing this, Quinn? You know we're good together."

"It's the right thing to do. We want different things and that's not going to change."

"Is this because of that SEAL guy?"

"Judson?"

"Yeah, the one you went to Germany for last year."

"No. This is about us being wrong for each other."

"He showed back up when the Colonel died, didn't he?" Jeff's voice is dripping with contempt.

"This has nothing to do with him. Yes, he's in town for the funeral and Ms. Polly, but that has nothing to do with this conversation."

"That's bullshit and you know it, Quinn. You've had it bad for the guy for years. Now that he's a cripple and can't go back to war he's ready to be around for you, right?"

"Why the hell would you say something like that? No, that's not the case. You're an asshole for saying that though. I'm done. I refuse to argue and listen to your insults. I've been honest. Can you say the same?

"I'm guessing you haven't spent every night alone while I've been gone. I wasn't going to call you on it because I'm not a bitch, but you want to act like Saint Jeff, let's just keep the record straight. You only want me because you want to break me, like a wild horse. You want to prove to everyone in the department who told you I was a hopeless case that they were wrong and you're the better man. You don't want to marry me for the right reasons. You can fuck off. I'm done feeling bad for hurting you, because we both know it's not your heart. It's your pride."

"Quincy, that's not true. It was only a couple of times. I figured you wouldn't care since you didn't want me."

A bitter laugh escapes me as I reply. "It's funny, I was just guessing about other women and got it right. If you love me like you say you do then you wouldn't want anyone else, no matter how long I'm gone."

"You're not being fair."

"Yeah, I am. Know how many people I've been with since I left Denver?" I ask as the sarcasm coats my voice. He's silent, unable to respond because he knows the answer.

"None. Not one. If you really love me, being loyal wouldn't be a problem. I didn't want to turn this into a fight, but I don't think it's me that you love and you're not going to make me feel bad for being honest. You can drop my stuff off to Gemma if you want. If not, I'll have her go by your place and pick it up. We're done."

"That's not the end of this. I understand you're upset, but give it a few more days and we can talk again."

"No. This is it. The end. Let it go."

I don't want him to say more. "Goodbye, Jeff," are the last words I utter before I hang up.

I sit without moving for several minutes, willing my body to relax before I finally get up and pull my shoes back on. I walk through the kitchen and snatch my purse and keys off the island and call out a hasty goodbye to Ms. Polly. Then I drive to the hotel where Judson's staying, circle the lot twice and notice his truck isn't there.

I roll out of the parking lot and drive straight to The Golden Leprechaun, hoping he's a creature of habit. When I arrive I see his truck and I breathe a sigh of relief. After I park in the empty spot next to his truck I take a deep breath and will myself to relax. Once I'm settled I get out of the car and hustle to the entrance. When I reach the old wooden bar door I pull it open and step inside and immediately assaulted by the pool balls breaking, a jukebox blaring an old country song and the elevated sound of conversation. The other night I was so focused on getting drunk Judson out of there the clink of beer glasses didn't bother me, but tonight may be a different story. It's been many years since I've had a drink, but there are times when someone near me has one and all I can think about is pounding one back. Followed by another and another. Times of high emotional stress make my mouth water for liquid stress relief. Right now certainly qualifies as one of those times. I'm not sure I'm doing the right thing by being here, but on the off-chance Ms. Polly is right, I need to try.

As the scent of stale cigarettes and beer fill my nose I keep telling myself to find Judson and get out of here. This is the last place I should be, but I'm not leaving until I see him.

It doesn't take long for me to spot him. He's on the far side of the bar again and as I round the corner about 10 feet from him, a buxom, trashy blonde approaches and climbs right into his lap like she belongs there. I stop dead in my tracks. If he kisses her, I'm out of here. I don't care what Ms. Polly says, I won't be the sad, spineless woman chasing after a man who doesn't want me. The closer her mouth comes to his, the harder my heart pounds in my chest. My feet freeze in place as I silently beg him, *don't do it, please don't do it.*

His head turns away from her and he spots me standing in the middle of the bar, and without a second thought he shifts his legs, dropping the woman from his lap so she tumbles to the floor. My eyes grow wide with shock as this plays out in front of me. The woman yells a plethora of cuss words at him while she climbs back to her feet. With closed fists, she pounds on his back and shoulder to get his attention, but he doesn't take his eyes off me. He strides away from her, to me, his limp barely noticeable tonight.

When he's right in front of me, standing closer than a normal person would, he questions, just loud enough to be heard over the music, "Why are you here?" His cheeks are flushed red and his narrowed eyes tell me he's angry I'm here. My heart sinks and an invisible vise squeezes my chest.

"Um... Polly, uh, you, ah, I'm sorry, I shouldn't have come," I mumble and stutter, embarrassed.

I spin to run back out the door when his hand clamps down on my arm pulling me back against him. The rise and fall of his chest is dramatic at my back. He pushes the hair away from my neck with a gentle sweep of his hand. His lips brush my ear as he whispers, "Why are you here?"

Everyone in the bar fades out of focus. I clench my eyes closed, gathering all of the courage I can as I take a deep breath and say, "You. I came for you."

"Why?" he demands, his breath hot as it flows over my ear and exposed neck. A warm damp kiss is placed under my ear and I shudder.

"It doesn't matter. I can see you're busy. I'm going to go."

His grip on my arm tightens as his other arm slides around my waist pulling me closer to his body. His erection digs into my back. *Is that from me or the trashy blonde?*

"You aren't going anywhere. Tell me why you came."

People are taking notice of what's going on with us, observing like we're a sideshow at a circus. "For you," I say, not elaborating.

"Tell. Me. Why," he grinds out, his nose tucked behind my ear. Ms. Polly's words come back to me. *Show him he's worth it.*

I turn in his arms so he can see my face and I say, "I came here because I want you. I have for years. Isn't that reason enough?" I want to tell him I'm here because I'm in love with him, but I can't. There's too much room for humiliation and he hasn't proven to me yet that he deserves for me to present my heart on a silver platter. For now I'll give him my body if he wants it.

Glancing around I wonder if I'm about to be humiliated anyway, but before I can finish the thought his mouth crashes over mine and consumes me instantly. His lips, his tongue, his hands, all of it. I respond with a passion I've been hiding for years. No one else I've dated has drawn this kind of response from me. We're devouring each other and I should be alarmed that I can taste the whiskey flavor in his mouth, but I'm too busy eating him alive.

He breaks the kiss when the whistles and catcalls get loud enough to penetrate our passionate haze. I'm a little kiss-drunk and dazed when he leans down and says, "I'm paying this tab and you're coming with me."

I don't question it. I nod my acceptance and follow behind him as he takes care of his bill. The next thing I know he's pulling me through the parking lot towards my car. "You have to drive, I've been drinking."

By the time we reach the hotel my nerves are live wires again, sensitive, electric, combustible. We get out of my car and he wraps his arms around me, pulling me in close. The parking lot is deserted so there's no one to interrupt this little moment.

"Are you sure this is what you want?" he asks against my hair.

I take in a deep breath, searching for his manly scent under the leftover smoke from the bar. When I locate it, I relish it for another moment before I answer, "Yes, I'm sure."

His lips meet mine in a frenzy that hasn't cooled since the bar and I forget we're in a parking lot until he lifts me and places my ass on the hood of my car and steps in between my legs to continue the kiss. His hand burrows up under the sweatshirt I'm wearing and grazes my breasts, teasing me. My fingernails run along his scalp, through the short strands of his dark hair. He shifts his hips so his erection pushes against me forcing my moan into our kiss. I reach between us and grip him through his jeans, causing him to groan. I'm thinking about the million and one things I'd like to do to him when I hear a woman's laughter closer than I'd like. I pull away and whisper, "Room, we need to get to your room."

All of his muscles relax for a fraction of a second as he says, "Okay, follow me, Daisy." My heart does a somersault at the old endearment. I smile to myself as I follow him through the parking lot, across the lobby and into the elevator. He steps up behind me in the elevator and slides his warm calloused hand under my shirt to touch the skin of my belly. His thumb teases me as it grazes the underside of my breast. When the door slides open he steps in front of me again, grabbing my hand, this time pulling me to his room.

Once inside, he shuts the door and slams my body against it. His mouth is on mine in an instant. Oh my God, a kiss from Judson Rivers is a mind-bending experience on a regular occasion, but too many years of pent-up sexual frustration takes the rating off the charts. He's devouring me. All lips, tongue and even teeth. This isn't an ordinary romantic kiss, no, it's like he's feeding on me and trying to climb inside me all at once. It's the hottest kiss I've ever had and I'm giving back as good as I'm getting.

The nip of his teeth on my lower lip forces my eyes open. He pulls away, panting. His cerulean eyes are hooded as his tongue snakes out and licks the sting. Before I can say or do anything, he grips under my thighs and pulls up. On instinct, I wrap my legs around his waist and lock them at his back. He lightly adjusts his stance for better balance and grinds against me. I throw my head back, smacking it into the wall and moan, half in pain, half in pleasure. I'll have a knot there tomorrow, but for now I need him to keep up the friction.

"Are you okay?" he breathes against my mouth.

"Yes, don't stop," I hiss at him and flex my hips. He grinds again and again, sending me higher. I kiss my way across his jaw and down the column of his throat, tasting the salty sweat on his skin. My mouth returns to his and my frenzy is more pronounced as I get closer to the peak. "Judson," I whimper. "Judson."

"Come on, Daisy. Don't hold back," he growls and grinds harder. I come apart, screaming his name loud enough for everyone in the building to hear and flop forward against him. He's rock-hard between us as my sensitive core pulses before he backs off enough for me to lower my legs. Then he kisses me again, this time pulling me toward the bed as he backs up. Our mouths separate as he stumbles over dirty clothes, typical man, leaving his stuff in the middle of the floor. When we reach the bed he turns and tosses me on it. I bounce twice, still boneless from the fully clothed orgasm he gave me less than a minute ago.

I take a second to peruse his body from his cropped dark hair, over his long-sleeved T-shirt, down his jeans and to his shoes as he removes his shirt and drops it. His pecks are perfectly muscled, as are his shoulders and abs. There is a little bit of weight around his waist but it certainly doesn't detract from the physical perfection of the rest of his body. He unbuttons his jeans and slides the zipper down slowly. He's commando and he's teasing me now. My eyes follow the happy trail down to the neatly trimmed dark curls at the base of his thick, hard cock. Sweet mother of God, I'm ready for that.

With his jeans pushed to the top of his thighs, I see a small area of roughened, scarred skin on the top of the left one, but my eyes are drawn away as his hand slowly strokes up and down his shaft three times. I prop up on my elbows and watch the show he's giving me. I rub my legs together restlessly as a new ache forms at my core.

As I turn my attention to his face, he commands, "Shirt and bra off, now." He's smirking at my obscene perusal of his sexy body. God that smirk! I don't hesitate. I strip them off and toss them to the floor. He groans and licks his lips. My breasts now hang heavy in front of me, commanding his full attention so I reach up and wrap my hands around them, tweaking my nipples lightly. He groans again and strokes himself once more. "Jeans and panties."

I squeeze my nipples again before I lie down, unbutton my pants and shimmy them down my lifted hips. He reaches out and pulls them the rest of the way off and drops them at the end of the bed. His eyes glide up my body and over every inch of visible skin. I shudder at his wicked smile and scoot forward, gripping his pants and pulling them down. He flinches and makes an irritated face, grips my hands and moves them away. Maybe he likes control. The further down his pants go the more scar tissue is revealed and I can't help but stare. It's the first time I've seen it. Even when I was at the hospital I didn't see it. I left the room for bandage changes because they were so painful for him. I can tell his demeanor has changed a little as I stare because his once raging cock is softening.

Afraid he'll stop this too soon, I switch my gaze to his and then I reach out and stroke his cock, encouraging, "Hurry up, honey. I'm ready for you."

Leaning forward, I swipe my tongue across his hot flesh, starting at the sensitive underside of the head, finishing with a twirl of my tongue on the head of his cock, and he returns to full mast. He backs off a little and sits on the bed almost next to me. He drops his pants to the floor and twists his torso like he's attempting to shield himself from my view. Then he removes his prosthesis and the fabric barrier that protects the skin from the plastic and lays them both on the floor.

He seems a little unsure of what to do now so I run feather-light hands over the skin of his back and watch goose bumps spread in their wake. There are scarred areas scattered around his back where the shrapnel was removed but he's still sexy. Even more so now. Probably because I know what he survived.

"Still the most beautifully muscled body I've ever seen," I whisper loud enough for him to hear.

He flips and crawls over top of me. Within seconds we are tangled in each other, our bodies skin to skin, his weight resting on me. My legs are wrapped around his waist as my hands explore the long lines of his body. My mind catalogs every part of his masculine form. I release my right leg and lower it to the bed so

I'm able to reach down across his ass cheek and as far down as the back of his thigh. The lower my hand goes, the more rigid his body becomes above me.

"Don't," he commands.

"Judson," I plead in a whisper.

Aiming to relax him again, I skate my hand back up over his ass and squeeze. "I want you," I say quietly against his cheek. He sits back a little and pulls a condom from his wallet on the bedside table. Once it's on, he stays upright and lifts my hips, impaling me with his length. His back bows and a groan escapes from his throat. I clench tight around him and lock my legs behind his back. He thrusts again, slower than the last time, pulling back, almost all the way out and thrusting again. The feeling is amazing and overwhelming. With his body still upright, his eyes watch as my breasts bounce with every thrust. He plants his hands beside my shoulders and powers in harder. When I feel him slip a little, like he lost traction, he grumbles something unintelligible, readjusts and goes back to making me feel good.

"Ahhhh!" I yell, and he does it again. "More!" I call out. His hips drive into me as I pant and beg for more. Without warning and with a little bit of awkward motion he flips us, seating me on top where I plant my hands on his chest and roll my hips against his over and over again.

His husky voice growls, "Faster, Daisy!" and I lose my rhythm as the need in his voice distracts me. "Daisy, please," he begs and my concentration is further blown. Realizing this, he rolls me to our sides so we are facing each other this time and slides his thick shaft into me on repeat until I scream his name again. Every muscle in my body locks up tight and I'm suspended in complete ecstasy. He pushes me to my back, thrusts a few more times until he lets go and I feel his cock swell and explode. His body collapses onto mine and I hold on tight, afraid if I loosen up or let go he'll be gone. We lie here for several long minutes until I get brave enough to release my legs and plant them on the mattress. I carefully explore his lower back with my fingertips, over his ass and down his thighs. I know he stopped me during sex, but surely he doesn't expect me not to touch him at all. The lower I go, the more tense his muscles grow.

"No," he barks at me.

"Judson." I try to calm him with a soft tone.

"Don't go there," he commands, his voice unfriendly. He shakes his head no against my shoulder and I remove my hand from his skin. His relief is instant as his body relaxes against mine.

"Look at me, Judson."

He doesn't respond and doesn't comply.

"Come on, look at me."

Slowly, he draws back from my neck as his infuriated eyes meet mine. He's angry. Not just a little, a lot. That makes no sense to me.

My hands move up to his cheeks, holding him there. "Don't stop me from getting to know you again, please. I realize you're not the same man you were all those years ago. I want to know this man, the one that's here with me now. I want to know you inside and out. Every single inch of your body.

"What's been stored in my memory bank is different than what I'm feeling now. You're bulkier all over, your muscles more defined, you have tattoos that I've yet to dissect and scars I want to touch. All of this is part of the new you, a man I'm insanely attracted to. If this was a one-time thing then I'll get dressed and leave, but if it wasn't then I want to be able to appreciate all of you."

He huffs and rolls off of me to his back, removes the condom, tossing it to the floor, and tugs the sheet up to his waist, effectively hiding his lower half from me. "I don't know if I can do this, Quinn." His tone is irritated and clipped.

"Do what?" I ask as my heart rate picks up speed again. My stomach knots at the change in his demeanor. I'm praying I didn't

I DIG my palms into my eyes, rubbing hard as I take several deep breaths and allow the emptiness to wash over me and seep into my pores. Why did I do that? She was finally under me. Sated, happy, ready for more and I sent her on her way. When I first saw her at the funeral, I told myself I couldn't pursue her because I couldn't perform like a man anymore. I thought she deserved more than a gimpy broke-dick bastard who couldn't please a woman. Even with the little stirring I felt when I was in her room that night I still didn't think I could perform. Then she showed up all pissed off and jealous and it turned me on, making my reason for staying away a non-issue.

I was hard as soon as I touched her in that bar so I practically dragged her out of there. When there was no awkwardness as I removed the prosthesis and no performance issues with one and a half legs, I should have pulled her down to the justice of the peace and married her right then. Instead, my insecurities with my new, scarred body reappeared and took over. I was a complete dick to her. I could tell by the sound of her voice and the rigid movement of her usually fluid body she was hurting as she searched for her clothes. The look of humiliation on her face was like a dagger to the heart. When did I become so vain that how I look matters more than who's around me?

What the hell is wrong with me? My throat burns as I fight the tears. I refuse to cry like a big pussy. I battle the feeling with everything I have left in me and tell myself she's just another chick, just another piece of ass. But my mind is a traitorous son of a bitch and won't recognize her for what I need her to be and it keeps drifting back to the things I did with her in this bed. To how I really feel about her. Little snippets, like movie clips, flash before my eyes of her splayed out on my bed: the silky feeling of her skin, the rosy tips of her amazing breasts, that tiny little strip of black hair that practically points to my heaven. I'm such a dumbass for pushing her away.

Breathing deep in an attempt to get myself under control, the scent of her shampoo and skin surrounds me as if it coats the pillows and sheets. The realization has my dick stirring again. Of course, after a whole year of lying flaccid, my cock's going to swell constantly now because I don't want it to.

I sit on the edge of the bed and scrape a pill bottle out of the drawer. I've kept it there "just in case" since I got here a couple weeks ago. I knew it was a bad idea since I was trying to kick them, but I thought I might need them at some point. You know, for the pain. It doesn't matter that I was supposed to flush them all down the toilet a while ago. I drop two in my palm and shuffle to the bathroom to get a swig of water from the sink to swallow them.

My mind wanders back to Quincy for a while until I finally give up, understanding there's no way I'll be able to sleep now. I grab the bottle again and dump a few more pills in my hand. It's leftover prescription medicine I was given for the leg pain and I'm thankful I hid it. I drop back down on the bed and lie there hoping the meds will kick in soon and help to dull the pain I feel at letting her go again.

* * *

The next two days roll by in a haze of booze and pills and I've finally run through everything I have in my hotel room. I'm out of pills and there's no way my doctor will write me a new script. I've been flagged in the system as an abuser so I'm shit out of luck. The problem right now is that I need to be numb and I have no way to accomplish that. I call the local liquor store and pay extra to have them deliver a couple of bottles of Wild Turkey. If I down another bottle of that, I should be able to get some sleep even without the pills. At some point I'm going to go find the guy who sells pills. John, the man who has been perched on the barstool next to mine almost every night, gave me his name, location and description the other night when I was in there complaining about being out of pain killers.

* * *

The next morning, I wake up, vomit a couple of times, shower and dress before driving down to the questionable part of town. I need to find something to take the edge off all I'm feeling. I grab a piece of toast on my way through the lobby, hoping it will settle my stomach, and then I get in my truck.

The whole way there my stomach rolls and my skin crawls. I can't tell if the profuse sweating I have going on is courtesy of the hangover or the withdrawals, but either way I'm soaked and miserable. In the logical part of my brain I know I shouldn't be making this worse by filling up on more pills, but the part of me that wants to run away from the nightmares, the pain, the failure, and the hurt I can still see lingering in Quinn's eyes says, *load me up*. It's the stronger part, so it wins.

I park in the lot of a run-down convenience store that fits the description given to me and pray my truck still has wheels when I get back. I find a scrawny little white guy sitting with his back against the side wall, knees bent and feet pulled up against his ass. The once white hoody is now grey from dirt and wear, and his raggedy jeans have seen better days. He's wearing a brand-new flat-billed Denver Nuggets cap and new, expensive-looking sneakers though. This is exactly how he was described to me.

"You Ray?" I ask the guy as I squint down at him.

"What's it to you?" His eyes focus on me suspiciously.

"John from The Golden Leprechaun sent me."

"Yeah, well you look like Five-O to me. How you know John?" He tilts his head and squints his eyes.

"I've been hanging out at that bar for the last couple of weeks. Need a little help. Doctor won't write me a new script. I need more to help me get by."

"Yeah, well I can't help ya." He rolls his eyes and switches his gaze to the horizon to the left of me.

"John said you were the guy," I insist.

"I don't know what you talkin' 'bout. Why he'd send someone looks like you down here, I have no idea. Tell him to fuck off when you see him again."

Ray looks away like he's going to dismiss me, which simply won't work. I need something and I need it *now*. I know this little worm has it, so I snatch him up and slam him against the wall, holding him there while he struggles to get free. I may be a mess, but I'm still strong enough to hold him still, and with my training this guy isn't going anywhere.

"Listen, you little piece of shit, I'm not the damn police. I got my fucking leg blown off in the sandbox and I need something to help me get by. John said you were the guy, so you need to pony up. I've got the cash, but if you give me a hard time I'll take what you have on you and not leave you a damn dime. Now what's it gonna be?" My spittle coats his face and the fear in his eyes shines like a beacon. I'm about to get what I came for. Inside I'm grinning. On the outside I've got my ass-kicking face on.

"Alright man, damn. I'll help you. You not the po-po? You gotta tell me if you are."

"No, I'm not the fucking po-po, but I am losing my goddamn patience!" I roar in his face.

"Alright man, come with me, but you gotta let me down."

I let him down and he tries to run so I snatch him by his hoody, yanking his body against mine, pinning him there with my forearm. "Let's try this again."

Ray sputters a bunch of swear words and digs in his jeans pocket to pull out a couple of plastic bags full of pills. "What kind you want?"

"Pain killers. Strongest you've got."

He sifts through the bags and settles on one while shoving the rest back into his pocket. He dumps several out in his palm and I shake my head and say, "More."

"You know this shit's expensive, right?"

"I have the cash, just give me what I need."

He dumps the few from his hand back into the bag and passes it over. I pull out a roll of bills to pay him and then climb back in my truck, happy that nothing happened to it.

I'm driving like a bat out of hell to get back and start my party-for-one when red and blue lights flash behind me. *Fuck!* Police. If that kid turned me in, I'll kill him when I'm done here. I pull my truck off to the side of the road and breathe deep, trying to calm my racing heart. I don't need this kind of trouble. The police officer strides up to the side of the truck and peers inside. Thank God I don't have the empty whiskey bottles in here.

"Driver's license and registration. You have any idea how fast you were going?"

I pass him both and answer, "I'm unsure, sir. Ever since I've been back from Afghanistan I have issues with a few of my bodily functions and I was just trying to take care of one before I ruined my truck." It's a fucking lie, an embarrassing lie, but I've heard guys at the VA talk about using shit like this to get out of this kind of thing. The cop looks at me and at my license and asks, "So the purple heart is yours?"

My eyebrows pull together and I tilt my head. How does he know that?

He must read the question from my expression because he answers, "I saw the purple heart on your license plate when I ran the numbers."

"Oh. Yeah. My purple heart." When the lady at the DMV saw my veteran's card she insisted I get it put on my plates. She said one day I'd thank her. If she were around I certainly would right now.

"I've been back almost a year and I'm still a mess."

He studies me for a moment and replies, "It takes time. Been there, done that. 10 years ago. Iraq." Neither of us elaborate further but it's clear we share something most people don't and for the first time I'm thankful for it.

"Here's your stuff. Slow it down. The next guy may not let it go with a warning. If you need to stop for a bathroom, go two blocks up and take a right. There's a convenience store there with a decent bathroom. Take care, man."

"You too."

Damn, I've got to settle down. I hate how desperate I feel. I'm just making more trouble for myself. Going the speed limit the rest of the way, I return to the hotel wondering what the hell I'm doing to myself.

Once I arrive back in my room I down some of what Ray gave me with the last of my whiskey. I decide going without whiskey is a bad idea so I shove the bag of pills into my pocket and return to the bar. It's mid-afternoon when I take my seat on the stool I've occupied for the last couple of weeks. I order three double shots of whiskey and drop those down my throat in quick succession. Then I order a beer and shoot pool with a couple of guys who spend so much time in here it's highly possible they live here.

A couple of hours, a handful of pills, three more shots and at least a six-pack of beer later, I park my ass back on the stool. More because the room is spinning and tilted than because I'm ready to sit down. With all the chemicals I have in my body right now, you'd think I would've forgotten all about my missing leg, my dead friends, and the hurt look on Quincy's face when she left me the other night, but that's not how things are playing out for me. There's a burning in my chest and a tornado of thoughts whirling in my mind, which I can do nothing to quiet.

A new bartender is behind the bar tonight and she serves me several more shots. I had a routine going with the other guy over the last couple weeks. Enter, drink my weight in beer and whisky, he'd call me a cab, I'd wake up and repeat the next day. It worked well for me. I wonder if I can expect the same from her.

"Hey, Jess, right?" I call to the new bartender.

She continues to dry the glasses in front of her but replies, "What can I get for you, hon?"

"I'm good for a minute. You new?"

She shakes her head and answers, "Nah, I fill in when the guys go on vacation. I've got a kid at home now so I don't like to work nights but they don't trust anyone else so a couple of times a year I cover for them when they need to take a break. It gives me some extra cash and a chance to get out of the house."

"Oh, well..." I trail off, knowing I had something to tell her but it slipped away like a fart in the wind.

"Don't worry, sugar. I've already been warned I'll probably be sending you to your hotel in a cab. The other guy left me strict instructions on what to do with you at the end of the night."

I nod and smile, glad that someone knows what's going on and will get me to the place I call home at the end of the night.

On my second trip to the bathroom I palm some more pills and swallow them with water from the sink. When I return to my stool I slam another glass of whiskey. Pain is so not what I'm feeling now as it all mixes to mellow me out.

The blonde who's been circling me for a week is back and climbs on my lap to sit. You'd think she'd have learned not to do that again after I dumped her on her ass when Quinn showed up. I guess she's just determined. Now that everything is back to working order, maybe my body will react the right way to her this time and I'll be able to fuck Quinn out of my system.

I don't think blondie realizes I'm a damn cripple yet and I don't plan to tell her. She wraps her arm around my shoulder and moves her cotton candy painted lips to my ear. She's whispering something that I'm not quite comprehending and licks my earlobe. I'd like to respond, but all of a sudden it feels like I'm hearing things from down a long tunnel. I continue to smile as she keeps talking even though shit's getting a little weird with me. I feel her tongue lick down my throat and instead of being turned on I'm a little annoyed. Which also brings to my attention that I'm not feeling right. My vision, my hearing and my equilibrium have gone from a little weird to way off in seconds.

I push her away from me, but she doesn't budge. She shifts and drops her other hand to my dick. I'm not even slightly aroused so I'm not sure what she thinks she'll find. Her nails scrape up the outside of my jeans as she purrs, "You're a big boy in there. Why don't we find some place more private for me to get to know you a little better...naked." She gives me a smile discolored from smoking, and the smell of her heavy floral perfume makes my stomach twist. This is a bad idea. I don't understand why this wasn't bothering me a few minutes ago.

"No." I push her away again, but she readjusts and leans into me. Persistent, sloppy kisses coat my neck as I attempt to get control of my body. It doesn't feel right. Not her, not what she's doing and not my body or mind in general. I'm way fucked up. Suddenly, I lose complete control of my limbs and I hear a scream as a falling sensation takes over. I hit the cement floor hard with my back and the room spins at a speed I can't control. John, the guy who's been perched on the barstool next to me the last couple of weeks, comes into view. "Hey, buddy. You need an ambulance?"

I take a few seconds to respond, hoping to stop this out of control feeling that's consuming me. "Nah, I'm good. Just lost my balance," is what I think I say, but it could be one giant slur sound as far as I can tell. He hacks an old smoker's throaty chuckle and helps me back up. Luckily, that maneuver scared blondie off and she's moved on to a guy at the pool tables. When I climb back up, the bartender shakes her head and says, "No more for you tonight, unless you want water."

"What? Why?" I ask.

"All I need is for you to get hurt on my shift. The insurance will skyrocket and I'll be out of a gig I need to pay some extra bills. Chill out tonight. You've got plenty in your system." I don't argue because my head is still spinning and the fall scared me a little. I sit on the stool for a little while longer in an attempt to get myself together.

When it's time to take a piss I stand and pivot, but trip over something and land face-first on the floor. It seems to happen in slow motion. My muddled mind fights to react, but loses as my forehead connects with the concrete floor. Pain shoots through my skull as everything goes black.

* * *

A beep, beep, beep sound rustles my senses. I can't place it. I know I've heard it before. I'm certain I know what it is, but I can't see anything, only black. I fight against the nothingness, attempting to focus on the sound for a few minutes, only to fade back out again.

I wake up later, slowly blinking my eyes open and looking around the dimly lit room. There's a light on behind me, but the overheads are off. The beeping I heard the last time is still there, but I can't find it. I try to sit up only to find my arms tied down somehow. I have no idea where I am or how I ended up here. The fact that I'm strapped down is not good. Thank God my training kicks in and I'm able to force myself to relax long enough to survey my surroundings and listen to the sounds of the room before having a total freak-out. The little drummer boy is pounding away in my head and I want it to stop.

Whispers to my right draw my attention so I turn my head to find the source, but can't see anyone. It must be coming from behind me. Why can't I see anyone? Should I speak up or let them think I'm still asleep until I figure out what's going on? More noise behind me. More talking. The language being spoken is heavily accented English, it sounds Middle Eastern and it seems like it's right behind me. I can't see no matter how far I crane my neck.

My heart rate spikes and I panic. I've been trained never to let anyone at my back. This whole situation is wrong. *What the hell happened? Where am I?* The beeps increase and I pull at my restraints as hard as I can. A growl escapes my throat, but I can't seem to say anything else.

Quincy slides into my line of sight with a worried look on her face. Her palm holds my jaw as she says, "Settle down, the nurses will unstrap your arms when they know you'll stay put. You have to stay on the IV and you keep trying to pull it out. Relax, I won't let anyone hurt you, okay?"

I attempt to process what she's saying, but it still doesn't make any sense. I tug once more at the restraints. Her voice and her touch are helping a little. I open my mouth to speak, but nothing comes out so I plead with my eyes.

"Judson, please settle down. I don't want them to knock you out again. I'm here with you and no one will hurt you." Her eyes beg me to listen. The sound of a woman crying can be heard but I can't see who it is. Quinn places her hand on my arm, but turns around to someone behind her. Ms. Polly is pulled into view by

Quinn's other arm. She's sniffling and wiping at her teary eyes with a ratty old tissue.

"Oh, Judson. If you needed help why didn't you tell me? I'd get you whatever help you need. You can't be this stupid anymore. I've called your mother and brother and they're on their way. They were driving back from vacation; that's why they're not here yet."

I close my eyes tight. Flashes of pills, whiskey, smoke, and a skanky blonde are jumbled together in my memory, but I can't seem to put it in any order for it to make sense. I don't want them to see the failure I've become. I hate that Quincy and Ms. Polly are seeing this, but it's my mom that needs for me to be the strong one. I can't handle her seeing me in this state.

Ms. Polly walks around to the other side of the bed, kisses my cheek and asks, "You think Gene didn't come back from both Vietnam and Kuwait with issues? You think I can't handle a wounded dog like you? Well, you thought wrong. I helped Gene and now I'm going to help you, but don't expect any easy treatment because you're my boy. I'm going to kick your butt back into shape. Now, I'm going to tell the nurses they can unstrap you, but when they do, if you fight, I'll kick your butt myself." Her face is fierce as she watches me for a reaction. If I wasn't so shocked I'd probably laugh, but honestly I'm a little afraid of this side of my frail old friend. Ms. Polly throws her shoulders back and strides out of the room.

I turn back to Quincy who's watching me closely, her hand still on my arm, softly stroking. The feeling is such a comfort I want her to do that to my face and hair. I want to feel her touch so badly. Words come out rough and gravelly this time when I ask, "Touch my face?"

She studies me for a minute and shifts her other hand up to my face, running her fingers and palm across my cheek and over the stubble of my hair above my ear. I lean into the touch and she does it again and again for me. I don't ever want her to stop.

When I open my eyes, I see the tears she has rolling down her face as she continues to stroke my skin.

"Why didn't you tell me you were having a hard time? This is bad, Judson. You almost died, you had so much shit in your system. You mixed a ridiculous amount of alcohol with a bunch of meds, none of which you had a prescription for. What were you thinking?"

I attempt to wrap my mind around what she's said and what Ms. Polly said, but I can't quite understand it. "What?" I scrape out.

"You took a bunch of pills, washed them down with a gallon or two of whiskey and almost died on the floor of the bar. Thank God the bartender called 911 quickly because your head was bleeding at an alarming rate and your system was shutting down. We almost lost you again."

Flashes of what she's talking about jump across my memory too quickly to hold on to. Quinn looks at me carefully, her damp eyelashes flutter as she blinks. "You don't remember any of that, do you?"

I shake my head and before she can say anything else Ms. Polly comes back into the room with the doctor on her heels. His white coat and pretty-boy haircut put me on edge and I tense up.

Quincy stops stroking my face, flattens her palm to my cheek and shifts into my line of sight. "He won't hurt you. I'm here, I promised you no one would hurt you and I meant it. You took care of me a long time ago and now it's my turn to take care of you. Okay? So just relax."

Her hand moves down to hold mine under the sheet and I do my best to relax.

"Mr. Rivers, I'm Dr. Janson. I need to check your vitals and ask you a few questions. Do your best to answer. Do you remember how you got here?" I look at Quinn and she gives me an encouraging look. I shake my head.

"Do you know what you took?" I shake my head no again and

then confess in a rough voice, "Some kind of white pills and whiskey. I don't know what they were though."

"How're you feeling?" He shines a light in my eyes and pulls back a bandage I didn't even know was there. His brows drop low and his lips purse into a flat line.

"I'm sore. Throat."

"Your throat is sore?"

I nod.

"We can get you some ice chips to help with that, but it's going to be sore. We pumped your stomach and all that acid probably left you feeling raw. How long have you been self-medicating?"

I close my eyes, ashamed everyone will have to hear this answer. Ms. Polly must sense my discomfort because she leaves the room without a word.

Quincy speaks up, "You've seen me at my worst so don't hide now. Just tell the truth."

"I don't know. A few months maybe. I stopped for a few weeks and started back up again recently. I'm still having leg pain and I'm not sleeping well."

Ms. Polly comes back into the room with a cup of ice chips and the doctor holds up his hand for her to wait.

"Let me get your vitals so she can give you the ice chips." Once he's done he tells me my blood pressure is still low and they want to keep me another day or two to make sure I'm stable. Then he informs me that the social worker will be in to discuss treatment options with me because they'll be required.

I close my eyes, dreading all of this. Not for the first time, I'm wishing the bomb had taken my life instead of leaving behind this broken man I've become. Weakness has never been part of my vocabulary and I hate that it's on display for everyone right now.

The doctor leaves and Ms. Polly feeds me ice chips until I'm too tired to keep my eyes open. Quincy keeps her hand on my arm or strokes my face and hair until I fall back asleep.

I wake a while later when there's commotion surrounding me and I feel soft lips kiss my face and hear the cries of my mother. I crack open my eyes to find Quincy in the corner talking to my brother. My mother is leaning over me, smoothing her thumb over my eyebrows like she did when I was little and had trouble sleeping.

Our eyes meet and she inquires as her lip quivers, "Why didn't you tell me? I knew something wasn't right, but you wouldn't fess up. Oh my God! When we got that call from Polly I thought I'd die. How could you be so stupid?" She's sobbing now and it hurts to see her this way.

"Mom," is all I can muster. I raise my hands to wrap around her as she lies across my chest. I'm so thankful they removed the restraints so I can pull her against me.

My brother glares at me from across the room and I look away, holding on to my mom as she soaks my hospital gown. Quinn moves over and slides a chair up for my mom. She pulls away and wipes her eyes as she sits. Quinn explains everything the doctor said earlier and my brother says nothing before he turns and storms out of the room. Quinn goes after him so it's just Mom and me in the room.

"No more messing around, Judd. I love you so much and I'm so thankful for all you did for your brother and me, but it's time to get your shit straight and start living your life for you. No more doing the right thing for everyone else. No more hero stuff. I want you to live for you. I'll support you through all of this, but you're going to get help. I don't care how hard it is or how long it takes. I want you to get help and follow through." She's crying again and it guts me to see her like this. I feel like an ass for putting her though more than she already has been.

After an hour she kisses my cheek and says, "I'll be back tomorrow. I'm going home to get some sleep. I love you, Judson."

"I love you, too, Mom."

* * *

Two days later I'm driven to Ms. Polly's house. My mom wanted me to come home with her, but she is still working full time and only has a one bedroom apartment so it was decided that I would go with Quinn and Ms. Polly who has plenty of room and nowhere to be. Apparently Quincy checked me out of the hotel and took my stuff to Ms. Polly's. They put me in the room across from Quinn's and are taking turns watching me and driving me around. I'm sure I can drive by now, but they won't even give me my keys. I think they're afraid I'll go for the pills or booze again, but I'm too tired to do that.

On day three, I'm dropped off at one-on-one counseling. The therapist's name is Dave and he's a Dessert Storm era retired Marine who went back to school to be a shrink. I guess if I have to do this it's best to do it with him. That's not to say this process is any easier, but it's required.

Surprisingly, the first session is about how I grew up and what made me go into the Navy. It was easy to answer those questions because I had an amazing childhood. I was raised on a farm by both parents with my brother. We worked hard but had plenty of space to play hard too. My parents were crazy in love with each other and in turn with us too. I was in my third year of college when my father died of a heart attack while he was out working in the field.

That single event changed the trajectory of my life. I dropped out of school and went into the Navy. My mother needed the financial help and my older brother, Joel, was knee-deep in school, unable to help her. It only made sense that I be the one to get a job. I always wanted to go into the military but didn't because my high school sweetheart and girlfriend at the time, Jenny, wanted to stay in our hometown. The day after I signed up for the Navy, I broke up with her knowing she'd never be happy with my life choice.

By the time I cover all of that our session is over and I leave his office wondering why he never asked about my prosthesis. I thought the IED and the missing leg would be the first questions. That seemed to be the case with the shrinks at the VA. I'm due to return to his office in two days and I'm no longer dreading it, so this approach of his must work.

On day four out of the hospital, I'm sitting on the swing on the back porch contemplating my situation when the door opens and Ms. Polly leads Jenny out to where I'm sitting. You could have scraped my chin off the floor when I register it's her. *Why is she here?*

"Hey, how are you feeling?" She gestures to the jagged stitches jutting down over the side of my forehead where I face-planted at the bar.

I shrug, not wanting to lie or to share the truth. "Hey," I greet her, "what are you doing here?"

"I wanted to see you for myself. Make sure you're okay," her voice is quiet and sincere.

I sweep my hand to the spot next to me on the swing and she sits, tucking her dress down under her legs.

"How are you?" I ask to be polite.

"I'm good. Staying busy with the kids."

"I bet." I give her a small smile, hoping to take some of the awkwardness out of the encounter. "How did you hear about me?" I ask and gesture to my bandaged head.

"I saw your mom and Quincy at the grocery store and they told me. Quinn didn't tell me you two got together. It's probably a little awkward for her. I've kept in touch with her, you know."

I didn't know they kept in touch and a sting of jealousy stabs at me that Jenny probably knows way more about Quinn than I do. "We aren't together."

"Why not? Isn't she here taking care of you?" Her head tilts and her eyes squint a little. "If you aren't then you should be. Don't let her get away."

"What are you talking about?" I give Jenny a look to let her know I think she's nuts.

"Are you that dense? After all this time?" She brushes the edges of her skirt down with her palms and looks at her hands for a moment before she meets my eyes again. Jenny's still beautiful in that blond-haired, blued-eyed, all-American-girl kind of way, but looking at her I feel nothing but a distant fond affection. It's really strange to think I might have married her if my dad hadn't died. "She's in love with you. She has been since college."

"No she wasn't...isn't," I deny.

"I knew it then and I know it now. I thought you felt the same. In fact, I thought that's why you broke up with me."

"If you've kept in touch with her you know that's not the case. I only wrote her one letter after I left for the Navy and didn't see her again until the Colonel's funeral. Well I guess I saw her in Germany, but I don't remember much from that time."

"She wrote to you though. She may never have sent the letters, but I know she wrote them. She flew with the Colonel to Germany and stayed for two weeks. She refused to leave your side until she knew you were going to make it. I know this because she was calling to give me updates."

"Why?"

"Why did she go to Germany or why did she call me?" she asks, confused.

I shrug. "Both, I guess." What a bizarre conversation.

"She called me because she knew I'd see your name on the news and freak out. We may not have been together, but I've always cared about you and she knew it. She didn't leave your side because she's in love with you. How can you not see that?

"She's never said it, but I suspect there was a time you were together and neither one of you told me, which is probably for the best. I was pretty raw for a long time, but I have a good life, a happy life. It's the one I was meant to lead and it's time for you to do the same. If you don't feel anything for Quincy please let her go, but if there's even a spark of something, I hope you grab onto it and hold tight. You both deserve it and I believe you were meant for each other."

I don't say anything because I'm not sure what to say. We both look out at the forest behind the house and swing quietly. It shouldn't be awkward since we haven't been together in 10 years, but it still is.

After a few minutes I ask questions about her husband and kids and she answers with stories about all of them with obvious affection in her voice. I expected to feel a little sadness at what might have been with Jenny, but like the day in the grocery store it never comes. Instead, I find that I'm glad I broke things off with her, especially knowing she's happier now than she ever would've been with me.

When it's time for her to leave she stands and leans over me, placing a sweet, friendly kiss on my cheek, and says, "Tell her how you feel. I know you love her. Just do it. You're not a coward so quit acting like one." She swipes the place she just kissed with her thumb and continues, "Take care of yourself. I'm glad you're okay, please stay that way." Before I can respond she slips out the screen door without another word.

Chapter Six

QUINN

THE JEALOUSY EATS away at my heart as I watch them swing together on the back porch. She's talking and he's laughing. I've always loved his laughter. He's a solemn, quiet guy most of the time so when he shares those rare moments my heart melts. I continue to watch them together, wishing it was me who made him laugh instead of scowl all the time.

Jenny's still a beauty. She's the light to my dark with her blond hair and blue eyes. She looks a little older but she's still stunning in a girl-next-door kind of way. Her curves are more accentuated after the birth of her children and her smile brighter somehow.

Instead of going to say hello like I probably should, I take my jealous self to my room and curl up with a book on the couch. I can't face the happy pair right now. I'm afraid I'll see Judson's regret written all over his face as he looks at her and I can't handle that. I'm still stinging from his rejection following our tryst.

Seeing them together takes me back to the night I found out they broke up. My cell phone rang, dragging me out of a deep sleep. The room was pitch-black so I grabbed the phone and picked up without checking the caller ID. Judson's father had died and he was back home in Colorado for the funeral while I was still in school. For the last five months, except for Christmas break, we were inseparable as he helped me get through my drunken emotional crap, and I'd become closer to him than anyone else I knew. I had a ton of friends, but none were like Judson.

"Hello?" I greeted groggily.

A sniffle. "He broke up with me. He dumped me, Quinn. What did I do?" A sob filled the dead air. It was Jenny, Judson's girlfriend from Colorado. We met not long after Judson and I started hanging out when she came to visit him. We hit it off and became fast friends.

"What are you talking about?" I sat up in bed and pushed my wild mop of hair out of my way. Luckily, my roommate was out for the night or she would've killed me for taking a call that late.

"Have you talked to him, Quinn?" Her voice quaked with emotion.

"I've called, but he's been busy so conversation has been short. What happened?"

"He enlisted in the Navy, Quinn! What's he thinking? He's been so distant since his daddy died. He's been worried about money and paying for school. I knew that was an issue, but the Navy? Really? Did you know?"

I remember my heart pounding. He hadn't told me.

"I had no idea. He did mention he wasn't sure how he'd pay for school, but that was it. We really haven't talked much since everything happened. He called two weeks ago to check on my counseling and make sure I was still going. The last time I called he was meeting with his mom and the accountant for the business stuff so he cut the conversation short and hasn't called me back. Shit. Is he really going into the Navy?"

She was blubbering and I wanted to join her. He'd become my best friend. He pulled me out of hell and helped me to stand on my own two feet again. I didn't want to lose him.

"What's he going to do in the Navy?"

"He's going to be a SEAL."

At first I breathed a sigh of relief and told her, "He has to pass a rigorous course to be a SEAL so don't panic yet."

Then it dawned on me that he was in excellent physical shape already, an expert marksman, had good mechanical skills and some electrical skills. If his mind held out through the psychological torture, he'd make it.

"Crap. A SEAL, really?"

"That's what I said," she wailed. "He got mad at me. Said I'd never understand. When I tried to reason with him, tried to get him to think this through he got mad and yelled at me. Then he came and found me a little while ago and apologized, but said he was going to do this anyway. After that, he said he thought it was better if we broke up so I didn't have to worry about him while he was away and he could focus on passing BUD/S. What the hell is BUD/S?"

"It's part of Navy training for SEALs. I forget what it stands for, but it's really intense. Just give him a little time to calm down and I'll try to talk to him this week. I don't want to jump on him right away. I know he won't respond well."

"We don't have any time left. He leaves in two weeks."

My eyes bugged out of my head. "What? It usually takes forever to get everything going before they ship off to boot camp."

"Someone pulled some strings and he's leaving in two weeks." She went back to crying so hard she could barely talk.

"Okay, give me a little bit to think this through. I'll call you tomorrow and we'll come up with a plan."

"He's flying back to Columbus tomorrow to pack up his apartment and bring his truck to his mom. You didn't know?"

"No. I told you I haven't talked to him. He hasn't told me any of this yet. He has to see me though, I've got the keys to his truck and his apartment. I dropped him off at the airport in his truck and figured I'd pick him up when he flew back. He may want to avoid me with this news, but he can't. Do you have his flight info?"

"No, but I can ask his mom and get back to you. Please, you have to help me get him back. We had our whole lives planned. How did this happen?"

"I don't know, honey, but I'll do my best. Keep in mind though that if he already signed his paperwork there's no backing out. He'll be in the Navy and you may find yourself married to a sailor eventually."

"I never want to leave our hometown. I love it here. I want to raise our family here and grow old here. How do I change his mind?"

She wasn't listening to what I was saying. "I don't know if you can. Are you saying that if he goes into the Navy you won't get back together with him?"

Her voice was sad as she responded, "I don't want that life. I want him to stay here and do what we already planned."

I blew out the air from my lungs and said, "Let me talk to him and I'll call you afterwards, okay? Just stay calm until then. I can't promise anything. If he signed the paperwork we may be too late even if he changes his mind."

"Thanks, Quinn."

"You're welcome. Now get some sleep. Bye, Jenny."

I knew when I hung up the phone that night with Jenny there was no changing his mind. I hated that he made the decision while his mind was in such turmoil, but knowing Judson like I did, I realized there was no going back just by what she told me.

After an hour of rolling around in memory lane, I go to Ms. Polly's kitchen and start dinner. I notice he's still on the porch and I know with the sun setting it's going to be cooler, so I grab an afghan and take it to him. He thanks me and I return to the kitchen.

Later the three of us eat without a word. Tired of hearing only the clink of silverware to the plate I break the silence by asking, "How was your visit with Jenny?" I do my best to keep the jealous tone out of my voice. Not an easy feat.

He studies me for a moment and swallows his bite of food. "It was good. She said you're the one who told her I was in the hospital."

I nod and focus on my plate.

"I didn't know you kept up with her all these years."

Ms. Polly watches us like she would a tennis match, her head swings back and forth from person to person, but she says nothing.

"Yeah, when you went to see her after you left Ohio she called me to cry. We just sort of stayed in touch over the years. I tried to back off at one point, but she kept it going. She's been a good friend."

"I had no idea," he replies, his voice holding a note of irritation I didn't expect.

I sigh, reminded that I went ten years without seeing him at all. "I know. You and I didn't exactly keep in touch."

"Jenny does seem to be doing well. Happy. She hasn't changed much."

The green-eyed monster rears her ugly head again and I'm no longer hungry so I stand and carry my plate to the trash and dump what's left.

"Ms. Polly, I'll clean up dinner in a little bit. I'm not feeling very well."

I leave the room without another word and go back to reading my book. Later in the evening I return to clean up the kitchen only to find it already done. I get a drink of water and retreat again. After I shower, I slip on my pajamas and curl up in bed to read. I'm at the good part where I don't want to put the book down when a quiet knock sounds on my door. I sit up and call out, "Come in."

Surprising me, Judson sticks his head inside and asks, "Can I come in?"

"Um...sure," I mumble and shrug. I take a mental note of the perfect way his shirt pulls tight across his chest and shoulders. Why does he have to look so damn good?

He doesn't sit on the little couch. Instead he sits closest to me on the edge of my bed. My brows drop low as I study him. His eyes are focused on the carpet when he says, "It was good to see Jenny today."

I close my eyes. I don't want to talk about Jenny, the subject makes my heart hurt. She may be my friend but I know how much he loved her.

"She told me a few things. Things I didn't know," he informs me.

I still don't speak. I hold my breath waiting to hear what the heck he has to say about Jenny.

"She said you wrote me all the time." My eyes dart to his, wondering where he's going with this.

"Did you?" he probes.

I nod my head, still not wanting to speak. I have a lot of pent-up emotion and I'm not sure how it'll manifest. I've kept a tight rein on it since he rejected me that night in his room.

"What did you do with them? I know you didn't mail them."

I blink. They're in a box under my bed, but I don't know if I should say that. I'm not a girl who keeps a journal but those letters were that for me and I think it's why I have kept them all these years, but right now I wish I hadn't.

"Are you going to talk?"

Shrugging, I reply, "I don't know what to say." I avert my eyes and chew the inside of my cheek.

"How about you answer the question," he says as he sits up straighter.

"What does it matter, Judson? You've been home for a long time; they aren't even relevant anymore."

"Not that long. Less than a year. I'll be the judge of whether they're relevant or not, now where are they?"

"Why?"

"Where, Quince?" His eyes are hard, his tough-guy attitude firmly in place. Normally I could ignore that but this time I crumble under the weight of his stare. I'm such a mess that it doesn't take much.

"Under my bed."

"Here?"

I nod my head.

"I want to read them."

My eyes widen to the size of saucers as I ask, "Why? Why do you care what they say?"

"I just want to read them. Can I?"

I shake my head. The panic is growing, buzzing in my mind like a swarm of bees. If he reads those letters he'll know I've been in love with him for over 10 pathetic years and although I didn't sit alone and wait for him, I also didn't ever really move on either. As I continued the letters over the years, they started to read more like journal entries. My feelings are laid out clearly in each one. I should have tossed them when I moved in here. I don't know why I didn't. There was no need to keep all of those. I don't re-read them or anything.

"Why not? You wrote those to me. That should make them mine. Did you tell me how big of an asshole I was?"

I shake my head. Humiliation burns warm on my cheeks as I think of the words I poured out on the paper to him.

"Well, no matter what they say I think I should be able to read them. I feel like I'm missing a big piece of my puzzle and something tells me I'll find it in those letters."

I shake my head again. "There's nothing important in those letters."

"Then why did you keep them?" Because I don't know the answer, I give him a blank stare. Maybe throwing them away felt like letting go of him.

He sits there for a minute with a thoughtful expression on his face. "Okay, if you won't give them to me then I'll just take them." He twists and lowers to the ground gingerly and looks under my bed.

"What?" I screech, sitting straight up, not expecting him to take them without consent.

"They aren't yours to take. Just leave them, okay? I'll throw them away tomorrow to prove they mean nothing."

"Nope. I'll dumpster-dive if I have to, but I'm reading those letters."

"Why are you doing this, Judson?" I whine, feeling both angry and terrified.

"Because I need to know what they say."

I sit very still, staring at him for a long time before I give in and say, "Fine, but you'll be disappointed when you read them." My tone is snotty in hopes of deterring him.

It doesn't even faze him. "Okay, should I get them or will you?"

"I will," I grumble.

I get down on my knees on the opposite side of the bed and pull a big plastic bin out from underneath it. His eyes widen when he catches sight of it. I carry it out my door, to his room and drop it on the bed with a huff like a petulant child. Then I stride back to my room, avoiding his eyes, embarrassed by what he's about to read.

"Thank you," he says as I turn into my room. I falter a step or two, but don't say a word. Instead I turn off the light and get in bed. I can't pick my book back up and I can't fall asleep so I spend the next few hours looking at the ceiling in the dark. The night that spurred me to write those letters flutters through my mind like a movie.

It all started when I picked him up from the airport when he came to pack up his stuff and leave for boot camp. Some things in life you just remember like they were yesterday.

I'LL NEVER FORGET how I paced in front of baggage claim until I spotted Judson. What I saw scared me more than the idea of him leaving for the Navy. His normally tan skin was pale and dark circles shadowed his eyes. It was obvious he'd lost weight by the way his clothes were hanging off his body. This normally very handsome, confident man was obviously tired and world-weary. It broke my heart.

When I stepped into his line of sight his shoulders slumped like a little kid caught doing something wrong. He thought he could avoid me. I didn't wait for him to speak, I strode up and threw my arms around his neck and squeezed. It took a second before he reacted by burying his face in my neck and holding me tight. Neither of us said a word. He finally released me and tried to wipe a tear away before I could see it.

He was only carrying a small duffel bag so I asked, "Got more luggage?"

He shook his head so we proceeded to the parking lot. When we got to his truck I tossed him the keys and climbed in the passenger side. He got in and shut the door, pulling the seat belt across his lap.

"How'd you know I was coming back?" His voice cut through the quiet of the truck.

"How do you think?" I gave him a look that let him know the question was stupid.

"So I guess you've heard what's going on?"

"Yeah, I've heard one side of it. On the way home, we're stopping at the diner for you to tell me your side, and then I'll help you start packing."

"You aren't going to try to talk me out of it?" Disbelief filled his voice.

"No. It's your life. I just want to hear what you have to say."

"Okay." I was not impressed with the one-word answer.

He pulled into a parking spot at the diner we frequented and we grabbed our usual booth. After a few minutes of silence, I asked, "SEALs, huh? Why?"

I remember studying his mannerisms carefully as he responded.

"I thought about it before I came to college, but Jenny never wanted to leave home and I knew we weren't going to be stationed in Colorado Springs so I decided to go away to school for a few years, then move back and marry her when I was finished. I thought that would cure my wanderlust some. Back when I had options. Now I don't. I can't afford school even with the scholarship from the team. My mom needs help to make ends meet until she can sell the house and the farm. My brother's still in law school and not able to help.

"This is the best way for me to have a future and provide for my mom. Not to mention it's what I wanted in the first place. Jenny was the only reason I didn't sign up straight out of high school. Right now the only things that make sense are making money to take care of my mom and doing what I want to do with my life. It's too short to live the dreams that Jenny dreamed for us. When I get out of the Navy, college will be paid for, if I want to go back. As for the SEALs, I figured if I was going into the military, I was at least going to try to get the job I really wanted."

My heart sunk a little but I fought not to show it. "Fair enough. Why'd you break up with Jenny? I thought you were in love with her. I mean you planned your whole life around what she wanted, so what changed?"

"Circumstances, I guess. I love her, I do, but I don't want the same things she does. I want to see the world and do a job I'm proud of and help my mom so she's not wondering where her next meal will come from. I should have fessed up to Jenny a while ago that I didn't want the same things as she did. I realized while I was home dealing with everything that I love Jenny, but probably not the way I should. It never would've worked out with her, but until now I didn't want to face that idea after so many years together.

"I've loved her for so long that the thought of letting her go so we could both get what we want was too painful. My dad just opened my eyes. I know someday I would've regretted it and I would've blamed her. I also know that if she were to marry me and move all over God's green earth so she could see me when I'm not deployed, it would've left her hating me.

"I never wanted that for her or myself. I tried to let her down the best I could. She may not be able to see it now, but someday she will. She needs to find someone who isn't settling for less than what they want in order to be with her. She needs someone who wants the life of a churchgoing, nine-to-five, soccer dad. It's not me. It never was and I'm no longer afraid to face that."

"Okay, I get it. Did you explain that? That's not what she said to me."

"Yeah, I tried. Maybe it didn't come out right." His eyes lowered to watch his plate as he swirled a French fry around in ketchup, never putting it in his mouth. It was hard for him, but he was right, if them being together meant one of them had to give up what they really wanted, then they shouldn't have been together.

"Well, before you leave for boot camp you need to sit down and have that conversation with her, just like you did with me. She'll be upset, but at least she'll have a reason. Someday she'll understand. Now," I waited until he looked me in the eyes, "why didn't you tell *me* you enlisted or that you were coming back to pack up your stuff?"

"I was afraid you'd freak out on me and I can't take another freak-out. My mom lost her mind and so did Jenny. I couldn't handle it from you, too."

"What about your brother?"

"I think he was just glad he didn't have to drop out of law school to help take care of mom's bills. I don't think he's thrilled about it, but he knows it's for the best."

"I'm not going to freak out on you. I'm going to miss you, but I get it. I understand everything you've said to me. I'm your friend, Judson, I only want what's best for you and if the Navy is the answer then that's what I want." A tentative smile crossed my lips to help smooth his tension. Inside, my heart was breaking. He was really leaving and he was going to put his life in danger in the worst possible way. I knew I might never see him again after that night. My stomach flipped unpleasantly and I forced another smile.

After stopping to pick up packing boxes at the local hardware store, we went back to his apartment and Judson spent about 20 minutes talking to Schmitty, his roommate, before he took off for a party. I stuck around with Judson to help pack. It was close to three in the morning when we finally finished so I plopped myself on his bed with a sigh. I was exhausted.

He dropped down next to me and asked, "You want to just crash here? I can drop you off at your place in the morning. I'm too tired right now."

I twisted my head to look at him, "Yeah, that works. I'm too tired to move anyway." What I didn't say was I wanted every single second I could get with him before he left.

He adjusted the covers so they were over me instead of under me and turned off the light. I felt the bed dip when he crawled in next to me. Even though I knew it was wrong, like I was betraying Jenny, I wanted him to hold me. I wasn't ready to let him go. He surprised me when his hand found mine in the dark and he laced our fingers together.

"You're the best friend I have Quincy and it means a lot that you're supporting me. I'm going to miss you."

"You're my best friend too and I'm not sure how I'm going to do without you here. You saved me, Judson, and for that I'll be eternally grateful. I'll miss you, too."

I felt his hand tighten around mine, but he said nothing else. I must have drifted off. When I came to I was smothered in heat and hardness and it took a second to remember I'd fallen asleep in bed next to Judson, but how we ended up with him half on top of me, I had no idea. I can't say I hated the position though. From what I'd seen, he had a great body even if it was thinner than it had been the month before. He had one leg shoved between both of mine and his arm was wrapped tightly around my hip like he was afraid I'd get away somehow. I turned just enough to get a good whiff of his cologne mixed with his natural scent and it melted me a little. I've never forgotten that scent.

His hip flexed and pushed a rock-hard erection against my hip and my core simmered with the idea of Judson buried deep inside of me. The little fantasy I had built up in my head before I actually met Jenny a few months prior, which I never thought I'd see to fruition, was bubbling back to the surface. However, I was sure when he woke up he'd realize he was dreaming about Jenny and run like his ass was on fire to get away from me. For that moment though, I enjoyed his warmth and the fantasy of him.

I'm not sure how much time passed with us wrapped up that way, but I felt his hand shift from my waist and move under my T-shirt, up along the wire of my bra, bringing goose bumps across my flesh. His hip flexed again and I pleaded with my muscles to hold still so I wouldn't wake him and scare him away. I knew it was wrong on so many levels, but I couldn't make myself care as his fingers shifted and grazed the satin of my bra cup, across one nipple and then the other. I let out an involuntary moan as my heart pounded against my rib cage, afraid he heard it. Terrified he'd realize I wasn't who he thought I was in the dark of night.

His whole body shifted closer and I felt his lips on my neck as he located the sweet spot right behind my ear. It's still the one spot on my body guaranteed to get a reaction out of me with the least amount of effort. I moaned again at the feel of his wet tongue trailing down my neck slowly. I knew I had to stop him. He'd hate himself after the fact, when he realized I wasn't Jenny. I didn't want to though, which made me a terrible person, a terrible friend to her.

"Judson," I whispered into the darkness.

"Quincy," he whispered back.

I whipped my head around, coming a breath away from his mouth.

"You know it's me?" I questioned in a whisper.

"Of course. I'd know your scent anywhere."

"I thought maybe you were dreaming and thought I was someone else."

"No, I could never mistake you for someone else, Quinn."

"I don't know what to say to that."

"Say yes. Let me make love to you, Quinn. I've selfishly wanted this for a long time. Even before you ended up on my bathroom floor."

"You had Jenny though," I protested.

"I know and I never would've done anything to hurt her, but it didn't mean the thought didn't cross my mind."

His lips were touching mine when he asked, "What's it going to be, Quincy?"

"I shouldn't. It's wrong and what about Jenny?"

"Jenny and I are over. Not getting back together. I'm not asking for forever, just for tonight. I want to feel something. I've been dead inside since you told me my dad died and I just want to feel...something."

I ran my fingernails along his scalp, through his short but overgrown locks as I contemplated what he was offering. I took a slow, deep breath and then answered, "Yes, make love to me, Judson. I've thought about it for a long time too. I just never thought it would happen."

Before I could say more, he sealed our lips together in a hungry kiss and I melted against him, allowing all the reasons I shouldn't do it to float out into oblivion. I moved my hands down under his arms and gently pulled up on his shirt. There were at least a dozen times a week I had fantasies of touching his naked chest. He sat up and disposed of the shirt somewhere in the room and before he lay back down he found the hem of my shirt and pulled it over my head. Then he reached behind me and unlatched my bra and slid it slowly down my arms before he tossed it to the floor too.

His fingers hooked into the waistband of my pants as he pulled them off me. I was commando under them so that took one step away. He yanked his own off before he lowered himself between my spread thighs. The feel of his heated skin against mine sent spikes of electricity straight to my already engorged clit.

I shifted my hips a little, seeking pressure. He released a groan into my mouth and pulled away from the kiss. "If you keep that up you're going to end this before it begins. Just be patient. I'll take care of you, Quince, I promise." His hand trailed down to cup my breast, holding it steady so he could wrap his warm, wet lips around the hardened peak. I arched my back, pushing my chest forward into his hands as I silently begged for more.

"You are so sexy, so beautiful."

"You can't see anything."

"I've seen you naked before so I know what you look like and I've never seen anything more beautiful in my life."

"When?" I was wondering when in the hell he saw me naked.

He nipped at my peak again and said with his lips against my skin, "When I kicked that fucker off you and out of my room the night we spent on the bathroom floor. I'm the one who got you dressed before you started puking. You don't remember that?"

"I don't remember anything from about the fifth shot forward. You got me dressed?"

"Yeah, it was really hard to do once I got a good look at these perfect tits and that sweet ass. I was hard for two hours after that. Your skin is so smooth everywhere and I've wanted to touch it a million times since that night, but couldn't. So now I plan to kiss and lick every single inch before this night is through."

I groaned, his words turned me on more. His mouth moved to the underside of my breast and he sucked deep and hard. I knew he was trying to leave his mark, he wasn't in an erogenous zone. His body shifted again and his hand slipped in between us, slowly trailing down, sliding his fingers through the lips of my sex.

"Goddamn you're wet, Quinn."

"Yes," I whimpered.

His fingers circled that little bundle of nerves slowly with the perfect amount of pressure as my hips rotated, following his movements. When I was just about there he slid his fingers further down and pushed two up into me. I cried out, begging, "Give me more."

"I know what you need, sweet Daisy, just let me give it to you."

I wondered what he meant by Daisy, but then his fingers pumped in and out of me while his thumb grazed my clit and all conscious thought disappeared. My hips worked to keep his rhythm until my body flew headfirst off the orgasmic cliff into the perfect abyss. I could hear my screams echo off the walls but I didn't care enough to control them. I clawed my way down his back, drawing blood from his perfect skin, but I was so blissed out I didn't care.

Suddenly the heat of his body was gone from mine and my eyes popped open, searching for him. I couldn't figure out if he was leaving or if he changed his mind or if I hurt him with my nails.

"Judson?"

"Yeah, Daisy, I'm here. Just getting some protection."

"Oh, okay. I thought you were leaving me here."

His chuckle filled the quiet space. "No, not even close. Just getting started."

His heat returned to me and I could feel the thick head of his engorged cock pressing against my drenched entrance. "Give it to me, Judson," I demanded, probably sounding whiney.

"Just be patient." I could hear the smile in his voice and I loved that he was taking his time, not just tearing into me. That was the only way I'd ever had it and I loved that he was different.

"Spread wider for me."

I lifted my legs and spread wider as he adjusted his hips and pushed in slowly to start. My greedy lower lips pulled him in tighter and clenched, eliciting a groan from him.

"So damn tight," he murmured.

His hips snapped to mine and I found myself so full with him it was hard to breathe.

I laced my fingers together behind his head and pulled his mouth to mine, devouring him in the most mind-bending kiss I'd ever initiated. I feasted on his lips and tongue like a starving woman. My hips rolled to meet his thrusts in perfect synchronicity as my moans tangled with his breathy growls. I rocked to shift us, rolling on top of him, riding him hard. Sweat rolled down between my shoulder blades as my breasts bounced each time. I placed my palms on the thick muscles of his chest for leverage and picked up my pace.

I was close again. I could feel the ripples in my sex as the burning pleasure pulled in tight to my core, preparing to explode and spread to all of my muscles. I was almost there. Judson must have had a different idea, not ready to let me get there yet, because he lifted me off of him. Whiney protests were all I could manage as he adjusted my position, placing my hands and knees on the bed as he mounted up behind me. With a powerful thrust he filled me and I shot forward with the effort. He hauled me back into place. His hands kneaded the fleshy portion of my ass as he slowed his strokes. He leaned all the way over, caging me inside his body.

"I love the way your body pulls on mine as you're about to come, but I don't want you to come again without me. Hold on, I'm almost there, Daisy."

He rose up again and pumped into me repeatedly as I fought to wait for him. Another minute was all I could manage. My mind shut off, allowing my body to shatter into a million jagged little pieces. He wrapped his arms around me and flexed against me several times as his cock swelled even further to fill the condom. He held me tight as he finished and then rolled to the right, disposing of the condom in the trash can by the bed. He pulled me up so I was draped over his chest, my hair splayed all over the place as I tried to calm my racing heart. His fingers sifted through my hair tenderly and I loved it as much as what we just did.

"I fucking love your hair, Quinn. It was the first thing I noticed about you when I saw you." I smiled against his skin and kissed his chest.

Curious, I asked, "Why the name Daisy? Did you even mean to say that?"

I could feel him twirling a lock of my hair as he took a few seconds before he answered.

"Because we have this huge field behind my parents' house that's filled with daisies every spring and they're so beautiful. They look so delicate, like a stiff wind would blow them away.

They only last a little while, but every year those same delicate daisies beat the odds and come back after a brutal winter. You are beautiful and delicate, yet resilient and strong at the same time. It fits you. I think of it every time I see you, but hadn't slipped in saying it out loud until now."

"That's sweet."

"No, it's true. I'm going to get out of this bed in a few hours and walk out that door, breaking my own heart, but you, my beautiful Daisy, will grow and prosper in the coming summer sun, stronger than before."

"How am I going to live without you? You're my best friend," I whispered.

"The same way you did with me here. Get out of bed every day, exercise, go to class, go to counseling, go to meetings and go to practice. You're going to live an amazing life and eventually I'll be a memory, someone who helped you once upon a time." Sadness laced his voice.

"That'll never be the case. You'll never be just someone who helped me once upon a time. You'll always mean so much more to me. I'm sad you're leaving me, but I'm proud of you for making a hard choice and following your dreams. Promise me I'll get at least one letter letting me know if you made it through SEAL training. I've read the stories so I understand what you're up against. I believe you can do it, but I want to know for sure. I don't want to guess. Can you do that for me?"

He's quiet for a bit before he finally replies, "Yes, I'll do that for you. You mean something to me, Quincy, don't ever forget that."

"I know. I feel the same." I really wanted to tell him I loved him and I didn't want him to go, but I didn't want to be like everyone else in his life. I didn't want to be another anchor holding him to a place he wasn't meant to be.

With nothing left to say, I ran my fingers lightly over every inch of his skin I could reach, loving the feel of his muscles tightening under my touch. We spent the last couple of hours before daylight whispering naughty things and making love. It was a feeling I never wanted to let go of.

When the first streaks of daylight entered the room through his blinds we got dressed in silence and I helped him load his stuff into his truck. We secured a tarp over everything in case he ran into rain. Then he drove me to my dorm and walked me to the doors. He tucked my hair behind my ears and kissed me so tenderly tears pooled in my eyes and my lower lip trembled. I wasn't ready to say goodbye.

Resting my hands on his chest, I said, "Go see Jenny before you leave. Explain why you're leaving. She needs all the information. I've only known you for a short time and I feel like my heart is going to ride away in that truck with you. I can't imagine how she feels after six years of loving you."

"I promise."

"Don't forget my letter."

"I won't. Keep up with everything we started and if that Marcus-douchebag gets anywhere near you I expect you to give him a severe groin kick just for the hell of it. Now, move on and have an amazing life. Thank you for being my best friend, Daisy." I smiled at the new term of endearment he gave me.

"Thank you for saving me, Judson. I don't know where I'd be without you."

"You're welcome." He kissed my forehead and jogged back to his truck, hopping inside. His hand shot out the window with one last wave as he pulled away. I watched until he was long gone, the tears soaking the front of my shirt as I stood there in the cool morning air. Sexually sated, but completely broken hearted.

As the memory fades I finally drift off to a fitful sleep, worried about what he'll say when he sees me again after reading some of the letters I wrote to him since he left.

Chapter Eight

JUDSON

WHEN JENNY SAID LETTERS, I thought maybe a shoebox with some letters in it. Not a giant plastic under-the-bed storage container. I open the lid and it takes me a minute to figure out where the first one is, but after that they all fall in line. The first one is tough to read, especially knowing how I felt on the other side of all that happened.

Dear Judson,

You've been gone for over two months. The Colonel says you graduate boot camp next week and you've done well. He also said he and Ms. Polly will be driving to Chicago to attend the graduation. I'm so proud of you. Following your dreams in this instance was not an easy choice, but I know it's the right one for you.

I miss you every day. Practice and competitions are not the same without you. I now spend the time I used to spend with you, with Denise. Although when we're out of town, she likes to party with people from the other teams and I'm still on the wagon so that's not something I can do. I've spent a lot of time reading. At first it was biographies about former Navy SEALs and when those freaked me out I switched to mysteries and romance. I thought I could handle learning about the things you'd be called upon to do, but I was wrong. Now I'm more worried than ever. I realize you haven't been through BUD/S yet, but I know you and I know you'll sail through the program.

I talked to Jenny today. I've talked to her once a week since you left. She still cries a little bit, but I think she understands better now. She'll be okay. I'm not so sure about me though. I never told her about our night together. I'm sure you don't even think about it anymore, but I can't seem to think of anything else.

Your old roommate, Schmitty, tracked me down and asked me out last week. I said no. I felt bad for turning him down, but I still can't imagine being with anyone else. Besides, I'm not sure he would've respected my need to stay away from bars and parties. I couldn't ask that of anyone, especially in college. It just seems cruel.

Anyways, I couldn't hold my silence any longer. I had to tell you I miss you and I'm so proud of you. I look forward to receiving the letter you owe me once you become a SEAL and get your Trident. Take care of yourself.

Love always,
Quincy

The emotions swirling around in my head like the contents of a blender confuse the shit out of me. I don't know why. This was written forever ago. I look at the envelope and realize it was addressed and stamped like she planned to send it and didn't. I wonder why she didn't. I pick up the next one and read it.

Dear Judson,

You graduated boot camp today and I could kick myself in the ass for not crashing it. I debated on it, but decided if you wanted me there you would've gotten word for me to be there. Instead, I'm waiting for the Colonel to return with pictures for me to see and hopefully a good report about your well-being.

We have a big competition this weekend and I've spent a lot of extra time training. I'm hoping he doesn't jinx it by talking about it, but the Colonel seems to think I've got the first-place spot locked up. He also says the national team has been paying close attention and if I keep improving it's likely I'll get an invite to join the team next year.

Well, I need to go. I have a ton of homework. I just wanted you to know I'm thinking of you.

Love always,

Quincy

I remember the Colonel talking about all of this when we went to dinner after my graduation. I remember thinking I should call her or write to her during this time, but things happened so fast for me and I got caught up in it all. I stayed in Great Lakes for another six weeks for SEAL prep and then was shipped off to San Diego for three weeks of Intro training. After that I spent another 21 weeks, also in San Diego, for further training. During that time, I didn't think about anything but getting through to the next day. There were occasions when a physical test would cause mental strain and I'd detach. It was at those times that I'd go to another place in my head, usually somewhere I'd find Quinn, but mostly I just fought to survive the whole experience. It seemed like every day someone couldn't hack it so they dropped out. I was determined I wouldn't be one of those men.

There were 20 more letters while I was training for SEALs. I can hear the loneliness in her words and the strain as she fought to stay sober on a college campus. Each letter shared a little piece of her life at the time. There were plenty of guys who asked her out and I found myself elated when I read they got turned down.

The day I got my SEAL Trident is when the tone of her letters began to change. It's clear as I read them now that she went from a feeling of longing to resignation. I wrote her a letter after I graduated to let her know. I also mentioned that I'd been assigned to a

SEAL team and would be deploying in less than a month. I wish I would've written her more.

According to the letters, three months after I deployed she accepted her first date since we'd slept together and although that's now been years ago, I feel like I could hunt the guy down and kick his ass for asking her out.

Dear Judson,

I was really hoping I'd get more than one letter from you. I know I only asked for that one, but I hoped I meant more to you. I secretly wished you'd feel compelled to communicate with me. It hurts to realize my feelings were one-sided, but I guess that's just how life goes. Speaking of which, the Colonel said you were doing well on deployment and although you can't communicate what you're doing exactly, he thought you seemed happy or at least content. I'm glad to hear it. It would suck for you to go through all those months of training and hell only to hate your job afterwards.

A guy named Lewis from one of my classes asked me out today. I almost gave the standard no answer and then decided there was nothing holding me back. He's a nice guy, good-looking and smart, so why not? He's taking me to dinner. I probably should have said no since I'm leaving for Colorado Springs in two weeks, but I selfishly wanted the company. I've accepted the invitation to train with the national team.

Denise and Jenny both said that I need to go out and act my age for a change. Being sober and celibate apparently makes me the college equivalent of the crazy cat lady. So we'll see what happens with Lewis.

I hope you're staying safe. I worry about you constantly. I had to stop watching the news because I had myself worked up all the time. I'll write again soon, though I don't know why since I'm too chicken to mail the damn things.

Love always,
Quincy

I move the box off the bed and remove my leg for the night. I can't read anymore. I'm nervous about what the next letter will say. I don't want to hear about her date with Lewis or anyone else for that matter. I turn off the light and fall into a light sleep for a couple of hours. I wake around four in the morning and start reading again. Thankfully, Lewis didn't make it past the first date. The letters over the next several months talked about her moving and national team stuff while sharing an apartment with a girl from Texas. It wasn't until I read the one written six months after she got to Colorado that I felt sick again.

Dear Judson,

It's been almost two years since I last saw you and although I still miss you every day, the ache isn't as bad anymore. The Colonel still keeps me updated on how you're doing and I still talk to Jenny, who, by the way, is getting married. It'll probably blow your mind to know I'm going to be in her wedding. We've grown close over these last couple of years so when she asked I said yes. She's very happy. Her fiancé is a nice, steady, nine-to-five man. He's exactly what you knew she needed. They plan to start a family right away and she's thrilled. I know you'll be happy for her if you don't already know about it. We don't talk about you much. I think she knows I fell in love with you at some point during our time at OSU, but I think she's afraid to ask about it. I'd never want to hurt her so I don't mention it.

A cop from here in Colorado Springs asked me out two weeks ago and I accepted. He's a good guy. He doesn't drink either so I don't feel weird about that, although I don't find myself craving alcohol very often anymore. Only in moments of high stress does that happen. Anyways, Mike is his name. Tonight will be our fourth date. His schedule is a little screwy so nothing has been consistent yet. It still feels strange going out with someone else when all I really want is you, but two years of silence says it all. My brain keeps yelling, LET HIM GO! My heart on the other hand says, hang on a little longer.

I have to be honest, if I could figure out how to let go I would. It's pathetic at this point.

Well, I guess I'd better go and get ready for the date. I will continue to pray for you and hope that you are well.

Love always,
Quincy

Why didn't I write to her? I missed her too. I thought about her almost every day. I wrote the Colonel and asked questions about her in every letter. I never asked about Jenny, not even when I talked to Mom on the phone. What was I thinking?

* * *

By day three I've made it through almost all the letters in the box. I haven't slept since the couple of hours I got that first night. I wanted to know what happened to Mike and then the next several guys she dated after that. I also haven't seen her. Ms. Polly came to my door to check on me and I told her I was okay but I haven't seen her either.

I finally crashed out for a couple of hours and got a little something to eat. Now I'm up to a guy named Jeff in the letters. This is the one who scares me the most. He's had the most potential so far and it seems he's working the hardest to keep her. He kicked up a little fuss when she came to see me in Germany, but let it die down when he realized she'd dump him if he didn't chill.

The letters she wrote in Germany were the hardest to date. She explains in detail what she felt like when she found out about the IED and what it was like for them when they got to the hospital. She talks about running her fingers through my hair and resting them lightly on the artery in my neck so she could feel my pulse. She couldn't hold my hands because one had been burned and the other had taken a ton of shrapnel so they were both bandaged in the beginning.

What surprised me most was she never gave up on me. Even in her head. It's like she knew I'd fight and come out on the other side okay. I wish I believed in myself as much as she believed in me during this last year. I was fucking pissed that I couldn't continue on as a SEAL or return to my team if I chose to stay in the Navy. I didn't want to face my life without my team and I really didn't want to face it as a cripple. Paper-pushing would never have worked for me so it wasn't an option to be stuck behind a desk. She never saw that though. She was certain I'd heal and find a new purpose, that I'd be bigger and better than before.

When I was hopped up on the pain medication in the hospital and told her I loved her, she said that she figured it was the meds, but it was obvious she hoped I'd wake up and tell her when I was lucid too. Of course I never did. I vaguely remember her and the Colonel being there. It's almost as if that was a dream. For a long time, I wondered if it was. I don't remember much until I was at Walter Reed Medical Center for a few weeks. By then I was a miserable human being.

I have to leave to see Dave for counseling so I shower, dress and drive over. Thank God the ladies gave me my keys back. It's nice to have a little freedom again. Dave greets me at the door and ushers me inside. We continue on with my story and the basics of the last 10 years. Just before we get to the accident, our session ends.

"Judson, I can tell we're getting to the point in your story where the accident occurred. I don't want you to dwell on it until our next visit, and when you come back I want you to treat it as a story you heard about someone else. Just give the facts and we'll move through it quickly. We'll revisit the tough parts at a different time. I just want the basics."

This shocks me. It seems everyone up until now has wanted me to get to the meat and potatoes of the story. They all want to talk about how I feel missing a leg. Instead Dave seems to want to cover it all. I allow my shoulders to relax before I ask, "Why is that?"

"Because what you're going through now doesn't only have to do with the accident. It's a combination of many things and I have to get the facts of your life to try and figure out what makes up the many parts causing you difficulty. You have to remember I've been to war. I know all about it and I know it can change a man, but I also know that war isn't the only thing that can change you. I just need to understand what your other things are. If we dwell on the war portion only, we could miss some important factors."

He's stunned me silent. I'm sure he's correct in what he's saying, but it's hard to believe that more than a bomb changed me this much. I'll be interested to hear what his assessment is once I'm done talking.

When I get back home I hole up and read the rest of the letters. It's the middle of the night when I get to the ones before the Colonel died. Jeff is still sort of in the picture and although I haven't seen his face I'm wondering if he's sitting back in Denver waiting on her. Does she plan to go back now? Does she still love me? Does she love Jeff? Does she plan to marry him? All of those questions run on a loop in my mind, but the only way to get the answers is to ask her directly.

I creep into her room. The moonlight is streaking in across her shiny dark hair spread out all over the pillow and her face is relaxed in sleep. She looks like a black-haired sleeping beauty. My heart pounds in my chest. Why did I spend all of this time trying to avoid her? Why did I push her away last week? When I'm with her I feel the same as I did when I was 21 years old and whole. Why wouldn't I want to keep that? I must be a fucking idiot. I was only planning to talk to her, but something inside me changes as I look at her lovely face, smooth in sleep.

Chapter Nine

QUINN

I GAVE him the letters three days ago and haven't seen him since. Ms. Polly said he left to go to counseling but she only heard him leave. She didn't see him either. I fell asleep wondering what he was thinking as he read. Somewhere deep in the night I feel the covers lift and the bed dip behind me. The squeak of the door opening is what woke me. I can tell by his gait and the fact that he took a minute to remove his leg that it's Judson. Cool skin presses up against my bare legs as my hair is swept up and over the pillow, out of the way. His strong arm wraps around me.

"You loved me?" The rumble of his voice rolls through me, breaking the quiet of the room.

I tense up, debating if I should put myself out there any further, but I don't answer.

"Did you?" he asks again.

"Yes," I whisper.

"Do you still? I've been reading the letters and I didn't make it to the last one."

I stay quiet, unsure of how to answer.

"Do. You. Still. Love me?" he asks, with a pause after almost every word for emphasis.

"If you won't answer that question will you at least tell me if you're in love with Jeff?"

"No, I'm not in love with Jeff. I care about him, but I'm not in love with him."

"Are you going to keep seeing him?"

"No, I already ended it."

"Why?"

I don't answer. I can't lie and I don't want to tell the truth.

"Is it because you still love me?"

I pause for a long moment before I finally answer, "Yes."

"Even though I'm half the man I left here as? Even though I'm a drug addict? Even though I'm a mess who can't get his shit together? Even though I've been a huge dick to you?"

"Yes."

"Why? You can do so much better. You're the most beautiful woman I've ever seen in my life. Your loyalty and tenderness are rivaled only by your strength. I'm not worthy of you. Why me?"

"I just love you. I have since the night you saved me all those years ago. There's just something about you that calls to me."

"It doesn't make sense. I didn't write you on purpose. So you'd move on and so I wouldn't have to hear about you doing it. I thought you did, but as I read the letters I realized you never let me go. When you dated that guy five years after I left, you tried to but didn't. When you dated that guy I just read about in year seven, you still didn't let me go. Why? They sounded like good guys."

"They were, but they were never you."

A soft kiss lands on my neck just below the hairline by my ear and my whole body shudders in reaction.

"You love me?" he asks again. His warm breath triggers a chain reaction of goose bumps all over my body.

"Yes."

"Say it." His hand slips under my short satin nightgown, along my ribs and up over my breast. He cups it in his large, powerful hand, squeezing gently. "Say it," he demands again. My blood heats quickly while my body readies itself for him.

"I love you," I say on a breathy moan.

"Yes," he hisses and his hand slips down over the other breast, kneading. "Again," he demands.

My core pulses to life. "I love you, Judson."

His fingers tweak the hardened bud and I buck against him. "Again," he says. His hand coasts down my abdomen, under the band of my panties and over my sex, cupping me roughly. I'm lost in the delirium he's causing my body. "Again, I said."

"I love you." I moan and wiggle against him impatiently.

"Again." I get it. I have to say I love him to get what I want. His little game has me so turned on right now, I'll play along.

"I love you."

He bites my neck and slides his middle finger through my damp folds while I pant and whine for more.

"Tell me. You know what I want to hear." His grumbly voice peels away any remaining coherent thought.

"I love you."

I'm rewarded as his finger strokes me up and down, over and over. And when I'm almost there he asks again.

"I love you," I cry out.

"Shhhh. Ms. Polly is home."

His finger rolls directly over my clit, swirling as he goes, quickly twisting the orgasm right out of me. I turn my head into the pillow to avoid screaming out loud.

"Turn over and face me," he commands. I flip without hesitation and hook my knee up over his hip. His injured leg slides in between my thighs and rubs against my already sensitive center. I roll my hips against him and he moans. His hand reaches around and fists my hair, holding my head still for him. He leans in and says against my lips, "I love you, too. Probably always have." My mouth closes the distance, crashing to his, my tongue stabbing inside his mouth without finesse. My need for him drives me wild. In return he gives as good as he gets.

I push him to his back and slide my panties off. Then I pull off his boxers and straddle his hips, slipping him inside of me as I lower myself slowly on to him. He groans loudly as I lift and repeat.

"Shhhh. You'll wake Ms. Polly," I repeat back to him with a slight smile.

"Sorry. I'll try," he whispers as he flexes into me.

I'm so full with him, I feel like I'll rip at the seams. His greedy hands pinch and knead the skin of my breasts as I move above him. "I love you, I love you, I love you," I chant in a whispered voice as we meld together. He sits up, bringing us face-to-face and I continue the rise and fall. My fingers lace together behind his neck so I can pull his mouth to mine.

"I love you," he moans back to me.

I drop harder on him, my arousal hitting its peak as I ride him. I grind down and ride harder to the point of my detonation. My core clenches him tight and my whole body shakes as a mind-numbing orgasm consumes me.

I collapse against him and he rolls me and takes a second to adjust his body into the perfect position. When my back hits the mattress, he powers into me as hard as he can. The pressure against my already sensitive flesh triggers another orgasm and I tense from head to toe as sparks fly behind my eyelids. He jerks twice more and empties himself into me.

Collapsing against me he says, "I love you. I have since college. I wanted more for you. I wanted you to let me go and find someone better, but I was too jealous to hear about it. I'm sorry I didn't write. I'm sorry I never told you how I felt."

"I tried to let go when I realized you weren't coming back for me, but I never found anyone better. It's always been you. I love you," I confess.

"I love you, too, Daisy."

He shifts so we're on our sides facing each other. His soft-ening cock is still inside me as he kisses me gently, thoroughly, reverently. God, I've wished for this for so long. I can't stop kissing him even though I know he's tired.

"You need some sleep," I murmur against his lips.

"I'm okay. I used to stay up for days at a time when I was in the desert."

"Why?"

"Depends. Sometimes it was what the mission called for. Sometimes I just couldn't sleep."

"You can sleep now. I'm not going anywhere."

He sighs against my mouth and buries his face in my neck. "Promise?"

"I promise. I've waited for almost 11 years to have you. You think I'd throw that away now that I have it?"

"Okay. Let's sleep." He kisses my hair and holds me tighter. I'm still awake when his breathing settles and the tension leaves his body. I love being with him like this. Please don't let him wake up regretful in the morning. I won't survive it again.

* * *

The weather is supposed to be beautiful today so we pack a lunch and go to a local park for a picnic. He doesn't have to be at the counselor's office until five o'clock. I'd love to go hiking, but I'm not sure what his current capabilities are. He was still weird about me seeing his leg this morning and things are so new between us I don't want to kill the high we're riding from last night. I already almost did that once today.

When I woke up this morning, he was on his belly, both arms up under the pillow. I was draped over him with my leg hiked up across his ass. The body heat he produces is off the charts so we were only covered partially in a sheet. I took the few minutes before he woke up to push it down further and study his exposed muscled ass.

Up until a few days ago when he started reading the letters, I know he'd been working out again and I was appreciating the fruits of his labor by running my fingers over the ridges and separations of each muscle group as I explored him. When my fingers reached his injured leg I felt his whole body tense and knew I'd woken him with my greedy fingers.

"Don't, Quinn," he mumbled, his face in the pillow.

My defenses jumped to the forefront because this scenario is what preceded me leaving his room at the hotel in a humiliated state not very long ago. I rolled away in an attempt to exit the situation. He caught me around the waist and pulled me back, tucking me half under him.

"I'm sorry. This is hard, Quinn. I don't want anyone to see my weaknesses, or the ugly remains of my leg. Especially you. Not to mention, when it was healing it was really sensitive, so much so that it was often painful. Now I kind of automatically protect it when the prosthesis isn't on it. The whole thing is a mindfuck. I'm sorry." He squeezed me tightly as I lay quiet. I had no idea what to say. "Don't clam up on me now, Quincy. I can't go back to silence from you."

"What do you want me to say? There's never going to be a time when I don't want to see all of you. The scars are part of you and I love you. I've seen you at your absolute worst. Do you think some scarred skin and a stump is going to turn me away?"

"What if you don't love the new me? I've done a lot of things since we were together all those years ago. Some things about me are the same, but there are some significant differences. The leg is just the most obvious change. I'm...embarrassed."

"You think I don't have an idea of what you did while you were in the Navy? I'm not an idiot, Judd. I've seen the movies, read the memoirs, read the stuff on the Internet. I have an idea. I get that I'll never know the extent of it, but I don't care. It's part of you, it's part of what you did for our country. Even if I were to see a complete list of things you've done over the years, I wouldn't look at you any differently. You're still the man who saved me all those years ago. The man who cared enough to help me when I couldn't help myself. You're the one who paid your mom's bills and wrote to the Colonel every week because you knew it made him happy. You're also the man who came to a funeral to support a little old lady when you had no desire to do it.

"Do you think I only see scar tissue and a prosthesis when I look at your body? It's still the most amazing body I've every touched and I've been with some serious fitness freaks."

A growl pushed from his throat as he climbed all the way over me and straddled my hips. His fingers linked with mine, stretching above my head. His eyes burned into mine. I'd pissed him off big time but I had no idea what part of what I said did it.

"Don't ever fucking talk about touching another man again. I'm not kidding, Quince, I'll lose my mind."

I took a deep breath, fighting to school my features. I was doing my best not to laugh at his surprising proprietary words.

"What?" I asked, trying to make sense of his sudden change. Feeling a little giddy that he may actually be jealous of me with someone else.

"The hardest part of reading those damn letters was finding out how many dates you've been on and how serious you were with each one, especially that Jeff guy. The thought of anyone else looking at you, touching you, fucking you, loving you, I can't deal with that shit."

I narrowed my eyes at him. "You didn't want me, but you wanted me to sit and wait for you anyway? That makes no sense at all." All humor slipped away from me and I pursed my lips as I waited for him to speak.

"I know it's fucking selfish. I can't seem to control it. I know I'm a dick, but I'm your dick." As if to punctuate this point he dipped his head to my peaked nipple and nipped at it with his teeth. Then he swirled his tongue gently to ease the sting. My back arched off the sheets seeking more. He shifted his attention to the other nipple, watching my reaction the whole time while I got lost in the feel of his attention and in his predatory gaze.

"Judson, dear God, don't stop," I moaned. He lifted his head and flashed me a wolfish grin. Then he spent the next hour proving to me that he owned every response my body could give. It was a fantastic morning. There was no more conversation about jealousy or dating.

We spread a blanket on the grass and eat while watching families and couples wandering the grounds, taking pictures. When we're done eating, we lie on our backs talking as the sun warms our skin. Things are relaxed so I test the waters a little by asking, "How's the counseling?"

To my surprise he answers without more prodding on my part, "Good, I guess. I thought we'd be talking about the IED the whole time, but we haven't even made it to that. He wanted an overview of my life and this visit today is the one where we talk about the facts of the bomb. He said he doesn't want my emotions or thoughts. He said we'll go back to discuss the deep stuff later. I can't quite figure this guy out, but I guess with this approach I haven't written him off yet. He's a nice guy, a war vet, a Marine, those guys are pretty tough. I get the feeling he's seen a lot so it's a little easier to trust him knowing he has an idea of what I've been through. I wish I didn't have to do it at all though."

I study his expression, surprised he's sharing as much as he is.

"I can't imagine any of this has been easy. You've never been one to talk a lot about feelings so that makes it worse I'm sure. I'm proud of you for going. I know you were given an ultimatum, but you could have chosen differently."

He doesn't respond this time, just laces his fingers with mine and closes his eyes. A few minutes pass and he lifts my hand up close to his face. It's awkward.

"What the heck are you doing?" I laugh as he tries to hold me still.

"Reading your wrist. I've wondered what this said since the day of the funeral when I caught a glimpse while you were washing dishes."

"Why didn't you ask then?"

"You weren't very happy with me so I didn't want to push my luck. Now hold still, you keep moving."

"It says, 'Find Purpose'. I got it during my time with the national team. I was struggling with what my purpose in life was. I couldn't figure out what I was supposed to do after that and I was ready to move on. I didn't want a job or a future that meant nothing. I needed my life to have real meaning.

"As a woman, it seems we're led to believe from an early age that we're on this planet to reproduce. I couldn't do that anymore so I didn't know what my purpose was supposed to be. It finally dawned on me that our purpose can change depending on the period of time in our lives or the circumstances we find ourselves in, but the important thing to remember is to always have a purpose. The tattoo is there as a reminder of a quote I saw one time by someone named Richard Leider. 'The purpose of life is to live a life of purpose.'

"Last year my purpose was to patrol the streets of Denver and make it safer for the people who live there. This year my purpose has been to take care of the Colonel and Ms. Polly. I don't know what's next but there will be something."

The little lines around his eyes soften as he stares at the letters inked on my skin. He lowers my wrist to his mouth and places a sweet kiss over the words. Nothing else is said about it but I can tell he's turning our conversation over in his mind.

After an hour, we walk hand in hand around the park talking about nothing and everything all at once. My heart is so light at this moment. I can't remember being this happy in a long time. I haven't been miserable, but I've not been very happy either.

As the time for his appointment grows closer, we fold up our blanket and carry our stuff to his truck. We hold hands all the way home like teenagers in love. I haven't giggled this much in years. The whole day was like a happy scene from a movie. If I would have realized this while I was in the middle of it, I would have been prepared for the black moment looming in front of me as we reach Ms. Polly's house and the scene changes.

As we pull into the driveway I feel Judson's hand tighten around mine. "Who the hell is that?" he asks, his voice reflecting the tension that crept into his whole body. I was resting with my eyes closed until he spoke. I look out the window to see Jeff standing with his back to the side of his Jeep, ankles crossed, arms folded, his eyes trained on the truck. The top is off of the Jeep, which explains his tousled hair. He's wearing faded jeans and a T-shirt. The look on his face is not a happy one. Shit. I'm not ready to deal with this.

When Judson parks the truck I squeeze his hand and say, "That's Jeff. I don't know why he's here. Do you think you can give me a few minutes alone to handle this?"

"No."

I swing around to face him and say, "It wasn't really a request. I was trying to be polite. Let me deal with this."

"Why alone?"

"I don't want a confrontation. This is already going to be awkward for me and I don't want it to be worse. If I go back to the department in Denver, I still have to work with him from time to time."

"I don't like this. Why is he here?" His light mood is long

gone, replaced by surly and uncooperative. I'm not prepared to deal with Judson's temper today. It's been too nice of a day.

"I don't know, I told you that. Just give me a few, okay?" He shakes free of my hand and steps out of the truck without another word to stalk past Jeff into the house. I climb out of the truck, shove my hands in my pockets and walk over to Jeff.

"Hey," he says cautiously.

"Hey."

"Where have you been? I've been waiting for hours."

"At the park. I didn't know you were coming so I didn't plan for it. Why are you here?" I study his features for a few minutes and think about what a good-looking man he is. Tall, broad shoulders, perfect five o'clock shadow, long legs, muscled body, and sadly it does nothing for me. My brain wants to focus on his thinning hair, lack of ass for the jeans, and his inability to take no for an answer.

There was a time when his charming cat-that-ate-the-canary grin was all I needed to see at the end of a bad day. A time when he was sweet and thoughtful. Sometimes I'd come in from being on the streets to find flowers or some kind of pastry treat on my desk with a cute note attached. That was back when I didn't question his fidelity and when he didn't question my loyalty to people who mean something to me. He never understood why I went to Germany with the Colonel or why I took care of the Colonel and Ms. Polly. He never understood that relationship and he became condescending and pushy when he realized I was going to take care of them no matter what he thought. I didn't like the Jekyll and Hyde routine. One minute sweet, the next minute a raging asshole.

"I want to talk to you. You can't think I'd just let you go after a phone call. I thought you'd call me or come home or something. I never thought you'd let it go like that. There's nothing going on with Marissa or anyone else for that matter, so there's no need for all this drama you've created."

All this drama I've created? Oh man! Not only is he delusional but he also just poked the dragon with that comment. My eyes narrow, "So you're saying you haven't hooked up with anyone since I've been gone?" He looks away and clears his throat.

"Yeah, that's what I thought. You can't expect me to believe you love me and want a future with me when you can't even go a few months without sex while you wait for me. I can't trust you. Besides, I don't think we're suited for each other."

"I screwed up, okay? I was lonely and I thought you weren't coming back and I...slipped."

He looks sorry all right, sorry he got caught.

"So you're saying that you were walking along, tripped and your dick slipped into other women? That's quite the balance issue you have, Jeff, convenient, too."

"That's not what I'm saying and you know it. I realize I hurt you and I'm sorry. I want you to finish what you're doing with Polly and come home to me. It's time we get married."

"No, I've told you before. I'm not interested in getting married. I can't have kids, Jeff. Why get married if I can't give you a family? That makes no sense."

"There are good doctors out there with updated technology we could look into. If that doesn't work, we could hire a surrogate. We have options."

"No, we don't. I learned a long time ago I couldn't have kids and have adjusted to that mentality. I don't want any kids, Jeff. I don't want to get married. I'm not interested in the white-picket-fence life you're intent on having. Go find someone who is."

He steps into my space so close I step back. He steps in again and grabs my shoulders, pulling me into a kiss I wasn't expecting. I freeze as I process what the hell is happening. I'm not kissing him, but I'm not, not kissing him either. I hear the door swing open behind me so I wrench myself away from Jeff and turn to find a crazy-mad Judson stalking our way.

"What the fuck?!" he yells, startling me.

"Who the hell is this, Quinn?" Jeff asks, pointing at Judson.

"I'm your worst nightmare if you don't get your hands off my woman, motherfucker," Judd replies as his anger fills and thickens the air around us.

"Your woman?" Jeff replies, incredulous.

"You guys need to stop!" I shout, pushing a palm against each man's chest as I stand between them in an attempt to stop an imminent, epic man-battle.

"I'm not stopping till he gets his hands and mouth off you," Judson growls out.

"Fuck you!" Jeff spits as both men push against my palms, moving closer together.

"Stop!" I scream again. "Judson, go back inside and let me finish this. I'll be in shortly."

"This is that cripple cocksucker Judson Rivers?" The nasty smirk spreads across his mouth as he backs off a little and says, "Then I have nothing to worry about. Quinn's hard to handle, she'll need more than half the man who came back from war."

That comment was like waving a red flag at a bull, feeding right into all of Judson's insecurities. *Damn!* Judson shoves me aside and lands a right hook on the left side of Jeff's face. A sickening crunch fills the air as Jeff staggers back, recovers and comes at Judson full force. They're going swing for swing, both grunting and growling like feral beasts as they battle in Ms. Polly's front yard. My mind wars with worrying about them killing each other and them trampling Ms. Polly's lilies.

Judson connects a powerful cross to the jaw, stunning Jeff enough to allow a second shot by Judson. Once Jeff recovers, Judson's sent staggering back, off balance by a surprise upper cut. I can tell he's going down before he does. He doesn't have enough hours with his prosthesis yet to be able to navigate a situation like this on his feet. He hits the ground on his back, leaving himself unguarded long enough for Jeff to jump on him.

I scream, "Stop, stop, stop!" I don't jump in though as they ignore me and continue to fight. I may be tough, but not tough enough to get between these two. Judson flips his torso, locking Jeff with his thighs and drills him good in the jaw. Then Judd grabs his hands, holding them tight. "Need a donut, copper?" Judson's eyebrows are drawn together in concentration, but his smart-ass smirk adds fuel to the man-battle fire.

Jeff growls, "Fuck you!" and spits at Judson.

"Keep that up, jackass, and it'll be lights out for you. I may have lost half my leg over there, but I still have everything else and if you keep running your fuckin' trap I'll make sure you know it."

"Judson," I call quietly to him, resignation heavy in my voice. "Judson, let him up. It's time for him to go."

"You want me to let him up so he can swing on me again?"

"No, I want you to let him up so he can leave. I'm done with this shit. It's time for him to go. Jeff, don't take another swing. Just leave. Please, for me. I'm begging you. I'll have Ms. Polly press charges if you don't walk away now."

Judson climbs off him cautiously, watching him the whole time, not trusting him to let it go. When he's on his feet, he steps back to block me from view. I push around him and say, "Go get cleaned up and I'll be inside soon. Just trust me." My voice and eyes plead with him. I want him to stop this and trust me. I know the kiss didn't look good, but I need for this to end so I can send Jeff on his way and explain everything to Judson. I can't do it with them fighting like we're on an elementary school playground.

"So I can look out the window and watch you kiss him again?" Judson barks at me. If he had a super power at this moment, I'm certain it would be flames that shoot out of his eyes to incinerate the things that piss him off. Right now, that would be me.

"That's not what happened. We'll talk about everything once he leaves."

"His lips," he holds up one hand. "Your lips," he holds up the other hand and smashes the palms together. "That's what I walked out here to see five minutes ago."

"We'll talk when I get inside. Please," I beg.

He grunts while dusting off his jeans and strides into the house without a look back at me. My heart twists a little knowing what must be going through his head, but I have to get Jeff out of here before I can fix this situation with Judson.

"You're screwing the cripple now?" Jeff accuses with all the venom he can muster.

"I'm in love with him, Jeff. Nothing started with him until you and I were broken up. I know you can't say the same so I don't want to hear any bullshit from you. You've done enough damage here today. Time for you to go. I'll have someone pick up my stuff from your place within the week."

"You're a piece of work, Quinn. Why didn't you just say you didn't want to get back together because you were fucking him? At least it would be honest."

"I've been honest from the start. I didn't think you needed it rubbed in your face that I've moved on. I don't want to get married or have kids. That doesn't change because I love someone else, Jeff."

"I thought you loved me." His tone changes and he sounds like a sullen teenager.

"I thought you loved me," I return. "If you really loved me though, you wouldn't have slept with anyone else no matter how long I was here taking care of my family."

"They're not your family, Quincy. You were just running from life."

"That's part of the reason I won't ever get back together with you, Jeff. They're not my family by blood, but they're my family just the same. The fact that you don't understand this concept tells me we never would've worked even if I'd stuck with you past your infidelity. Goodbye, Jeff. We're done. Don't come back. If I have anything of yours I'll send it when I have Gemma pick up my stuff." I don't want to wait for any more of his verbal jabs so I turn and march into the house.

Judson's not in the living room, or kitchen, or the back porch, so I hustle to his room and knock on the closed door. He doesn't answer, but I can hear him moving around inside. Screw this, I'm not waiting. I open the door to find him pulling on clean jeans. He must have gotten a quick shower. There are a few scratches and a bruise blooming on his face, but the dirt and blood are gone.

"Judson," I say. He ignores me and continues to get dressed.

"Judson, talk to me."

He sits on the edge of the bed and yanks his sneakers on and stands. His gaze is cold as it locks with mine. Gone is the warmth of the afternoon and the light happiness I felt all day.

"What's going through your head?" I ask.

"You let that asshole put his mouth on you!" His muscles are coiled tight. He reminds me of a snake preparing to strike.

I use a deceptively calm voice when I reply, "I didn't allow it. I was shocked and didn't react. I was stopping it as you came out."

"Yeah, I bet getting caught ruined the moment."

I'd love to slap some sense into him, especially after his comment, but instead I say, "There was no moment."

"That's not how it looked to me." He steps around me and pulls the door open.

"Judson, please don't leave angry. Let's talk."

"I have an appointment to talk to someone else." He leaves the room in a huff and I hear the front door slam followed by the door to his truck. Thank goodness Ms. Polly is with her lady friends today. I would have died of embarrassment if she saw any of what went on here just now.

I pick up his discarded clothes off the floor, pulling the T-shirt to my nose. I take a big whiff and close my eyes, allowing the smell of Judson to relax me. Even in college when we were just friends, the smell of him when he'd hug me, or when I'd sleep against his shoulder on the bus rides to competitions, or even just sitting in close quarters in his truck would always calm me. I was so high-strung during that period in my life. I lived for those moments when his scent would overtake me and work as a natural relaxer.

I combine his clothes with mine and run a load of laundry. Then I take my book to the back porch and read while I wait for him to return, praying the whole time that he won't find a bar between the counselor and home. I'm also hoping he'll be calm enough to talk to me and hear me out.

Chapter Ten

JUDSON

I ARRIVE at the counselor's office pissed as hell. Every muscle in my body is strung tight. I'd like to pound a little more on someone, but since that's not an option I guess I'll sit on the couch and get my head shrunk.

Dave opens the door to usher me in. His eyes sweep me from head to toe and his brows hit his hairline. "I think we may have to skip what was on the agenda and cover new material." His voice holds a light tone, but I can tell by the look that crosses his face he understands how tightly wound I am at this moment.

"Have a seat, Judson." He waves his hand at the wingback chair on the other side of the room. I sit down, my body dwarfing the chair.

"So, I can tell something is going on. Let's forget everything else this visit was supposed to entail and talk about what's going on right now with you."

"I got in a fight." I sit, waiting for his judgment, but find none.

"Go on. Start from the beginning." He sets the pen and pad he usually takes notes with on his lap and steeples his fingers in front of his lips, waiting for me to tell him.

"I don't know where to start."

"Who did you fight?"

"My girlfriend's ex."

"I wasn't aware you had a girlfriend."

"It's new. Well...not new. It's old. Well...not old. We're old friends. From college. Her name is Quincy."

I give him the Cliffs Notes version of my relationship with Quincy, dating all the way back to the beginning. Once I'm finished he asks, "You got in a fight? A physical altercation?"

"Yeah, he had his hands and lips on her, which started it and then he called me a cripple, told me that I wasn't man enough for a woman like her because I came back from war half a man. I lost it. It was a good fight. My balance isn't great so I ended up on my back but in the end I kicked his ass."

"Did it feel good to release some of what's built up inside?"

What? His question surprises me. I didn't expect him to ask that. I nod because honestly it felt really good to hit that asshole.

"Does this guy live here in town?"

"No, he's a cop out of Denver. So is Quinn, it's how they met."

"You assaulted a cop?"

"No, I assaulted a man who had his mouth on my woman. He just happens to be a cop."

"Okay. I won't touch that statement for the moment. Do you think she still wants him?"

"I don't know. He has both legs and no visible scars I could see. He's a cop with a future and I'm a drunken loser with no clue how to run my life. It's not looking good for me."

"Where is she now?" He looks up at me as his long skinny fingers grip his pen again, ready to take notes.

"When I left, she was still at the house where we're staying."

"Where was the cop?" His eyes hold mine for several long seconds.

"He left before I did."

"If you could go back in time would you change it?"

"No, I'd never regret her."

"Not her. The fight with the cop."

Shaking my head, I answer, "Oh. No, that douchebag deserved it."

He sets his pen down and asks, "So, why do you look so mad?"

I exhale and let my head fall to the back of the chair. I close my eyes as I sort through the jumbled mess of shit in my head. "Because I wonder if the asshole is right. I wonder if he's better for her, can give her more, can take care of her better. I'm a broken man, both inside and out, and she deserves better. So much better." I chew on the inside of my lip as I shift my focus from him to the seam of my jeans.

"What does she have to say about the whole thing?"

"I don't know. She said she didn't kiss him back. Then I left." I shrug.

He leans forward with his elbows to his knees. "Judson, you need to talk to her and listen to what she says. Really listen. Relationships are complicated in the best of circumstances, but with how closed off you are emotionally, it could be even worse. Does she know about the prescriptions and alcohol?"

"Yes. She had her own issues when we were in college. I think I mentioned that. She's been clean and sober for almost 11 years. She's encouraging me to get help. She understands all of that and even seems to have a good handle on me in this messy emotional place I'm caught in. I can't give up the chance to have her this time. I'm afraid though that I fucked it up by getting in the fight."

"The key to any relationship is communication. I realize it's not your forte, but if you want this to work, you'll have to figure out a way to talk to her and share your feelings. No relationship can grow without talking through the rough stuff and listening to the other person. It's very important that you work on this. My primary concern is to help you cope with your new reality, without drugs and alcohol. I'm here to help you express your feelings, instead of suppressing them, and to encourage you to make plans for the future. It's hard to move away from the past without a clear vision of what's ahead. At the next visit, we'll briefly revisit today so I can keep a handle on how things are progressing. Then we'll continue with the story of the accident. Once we've covered it all, we'll dig in deeper to the important things I see that need to be dealt with.

"For now, I want you to start with better communication. With your mom, with Quincy, your brother and whoever else is in your life. Try saying what you feel out loud instead of being stoic and quiet. It doesn't make you a pussy to have and share feelings. Even big bad war vets like us need to let it out and the people in our lives who matter the most need to hear it. I learned that the hard way from my wife.

"The best quote I can give you is not one of mine. It comes from one of my favorite movies and it's perfect for you and your situation. 'Get busy living or get busy dying' It's actually from *The Shawshank Redemption* but I'm sure you can see how that applies to you. Every time you're faced with a scenario where you want to retreat emotionally I want you to repeat that to yourself. I know you want to live. It's time you show it to everyone else, including yourself."

He places the pen and paper on the little table to his right. "One more thing. If everything you've told me about Quincy is accurate then she doesn't need you to take care of her. She's taken care of herself for years. Think about it." He stands and says, "I'll see you on Monday."

I stride out of his office to the safety of my truck. I know he's right. If I want things to work with Quinn, I have to open up and figure out a way to express myself that doesn't leave me looking like a caveman. I hated the look on her face tonight as I left the house. Now that I've settled down I realize she didn't do anything wrong, but looking out to see his mouth connected to hers had me seeing a shade of red I didn't know existed. I just wanted to end him so I didn't have to look at his smug face again or worry about his return. If her voice wasn't screaming for me to stop, I'm not sure I would have.

The guy is a total dick. She can do much better than him even if it isn't me, but there's not going to be anyone else. She's mine. I've fantasized about her for years and I'm not about to give up now because that jerk showed up trying to get her back. If I were a better man I'd give her up so she can have a man who isn't broken, both inside and out. I'm not a better man though. I'm a selfish bastard and I'll keep her as long as she'll let me.

When I pull back into the driveway I find the porch light on and the garage door closed. Ms. Polly must be home now. I'm nervous she's heard all about the little brawl in her yard today and I'm not sure how she'll take the news. I throw my shoulders back and limp my way into the house. That little skirmish earlier left me with a more pronounced limp than usual and it's pissing me off.

The sound of voices is coming from the kitchen and when I enter the room Quinn and Ms. Polly stop talking and look at me. Quinn watches me with weary eyes, but doesn't say a word. I can't tell if she's afraid of me or mad at me. Ms. Polly's expression is very easy to read. She's pissed. I open my mouth to say hello and Ms. Polly's hand comes up to stop me.

"Don't say a word, Judson Rivers. I'm going to talk and you're going to listen." She glances at Quinn. "Can you excuse us, Quincy? I'd like to speak with him in private."

Quinn nods her head once and rounds the counter, passing me in the doorway. I grab her arm to stop her. When her eyes meet mine, I see the hurt and confusion swirling behind them and I can't take the feeling it gives me so I pull her into my body and hug her tight. I place a gentle kiss on her hair and let her go. She doesn't look at me again as she hurries down the hall. I watch until she's closed herself into her room.

Ms. Polly asks, "Are you hungry?"

I nod, wary, "A little, I guess." The calm before the storm is a scary place to be with women, and that's definitely where I am in this scenario, sitting in the calm.

"Well, you need to eat. Let me warm a plate up for you and then we're going to chat."

I don't argue. I open the refrigerator, pull out some Tupperware and scoop the contents onto a plate. She puts it in the microwave, pours me a glass of milk and sets it on the table. Once the food is ready, I remove it from the microwave and sit down. She plants herself across from me and asks, "Are you a damn fool, boy?"

My eyes widen and I sit up straight. I chew my food and swallow, ready to ask what exactly she's referring too. I don't think I've ever heard her cuss before. This ought to be interesting.

"Don't answer that. It was rhetorical. The answer is yes, you're a damn fool. It's not the fighting I'm talking about either." She leans back in her chair and crosses her arms over her chest.

I tilt my head, confused by what she's referring to, and her eyes narrow on me.

"Don't act like you don't know what I'm talking about. I'm not mad about the fight. Jeff had that coming. Gene and I have never been big fans of his. I almost wish I'd been here to see you kick his butt. I'll just have to watch the playback on the security footage." She chuckles a little and then clears her throat before she gets back on track. "If you don't get your stuff straight you're going to lose the best thing that's ever happened to you." She points in the direction of Quinn's room and continues, "That girl was made for you and you know it. You should tell her every day that you love her and all the reasons why. You should take her out to eat and buy her flowers and shower her with presents. She deserves everything. Most of all, you should give her your heart. She needs that."

"I don't know how," I confess in a low voice, ashamed that I have no idea how to do that. "I've never been good with this kind of stuff, but I don't want to lose her." I can't even look at Ms. Polly as I share this. My face burns with shame as I stare at my plate.

"Let me tell you a little something about that old tough-as-nails husband of mine. He never sent me flowers. He rarely bought me jewelry. He never took me dancing or to fancy romantic dinners, but every day he was home he left me a little note taped to the mirror, telling me one thing he loved about me. He did it all the way up until the day before he died. He had to have Quincy put them up there toward the end, but he still wrote them. Over the years there were repeats, but it didn't matter. It was more the commitment it took to do such a simple little thing for me, and the idea that every day he thought of something he loved about me. It's all I ever needed in the way of romance. He was like you, terrible about sharing his feelings out loud, but he could write them. When he was deployed I got lovely romantic letters from him once a week and at the bottom of the letter would be a list of things he loved about me. Again, he showed the commitment and the thought. When he was home he never missed a chance to kiss me or hold my hand. It's the little things that count with you tough guys. I don't care if you steal his idea or you find your own, but you'd better figure out something."

I nod. "I'll work on it."

She reaches over and pats my hand, gifting me with a motherly smile. "I know you will. Now tell me about clocking that jerk in the face. Quincy said she thinks his nose is broken." I can't help but laugh at Ms. Polly. It's obvious she's never used those exact words before and they were hilarious coming out of her mouth. She probably heard them on one of her soap operas or something. She looks thrilled by the notion of Jeff having a broken nose.

"Yeah, I'm pretty sure it's broken. I heard the crunch. I think there's blood on my shirt. I probably need to wash it." She squeezes my hand and removes my dirty plate.

"Quincy already washed it." She winks and shuffles to the sink.

I hobble over to where she's washing my dish and kiss her wrinkled cheek. "Thank you for the advice and dinner. I'm going to take her out for a little while. Don't wait up."

My hip is becoming more sore by the minute so I stop in the bathroom to take some Tylenol, praying it will take the edge off the pain. Then I knock on Quincy's door.

"Come in," she calls to me. I peek my head in and ask, "Can you slip on some shoes and take a ride with me?" She stares at me. I wiggle my fingers at her. "Come on, Quinn. We need to talk and I want to show you something." She releases a heavy breath and sets her book down.

Ten minutes later we're in my truck driving down a dark country road. When we reach an old barn I turn left down a narrow trail and drive a quarter mile into an abandoned field. I stop and turn off the truck. I open the door and climb out, round the hood and open the passenger door for her. It's so dark I can barely see in front of me. It's a new moon tonight so it's even darker than usual. I help her down. She doesn't say anything but latches onto my arm with a death grip I didn't realize she was capable of. I lead her to the back of my truck, drop the tailgate and spread out the blanket we used for our picnic earlier. Then I lift her into the bed and climb up beside her to lie down.

"Lie next to me, Quinn. I need to talk to you." She lies down but leaves space between us. I don't like it so I work to change it.

"I think you know how difficult sharing is for me. I need to be touching you while I talk so I can feel your reactions."

She sits up and adjusts her body. Then settles her neck on my outstretched arm, looking up at the stars like I am. Her shoulder and arm are pressed up against my side and I can feel the subtle movement of her body as she breathes.

"I grew up in a house where the men didn't talk about feelings. My dad was a man's man, a hard worker, a good dad and a good husband. He just wasn't one to promote the sharing of feelings amongst men. He felt like working hard and taking care of us should be all that was necessary to explain how he felt about the people he loved. I'd never known a man who told the woman he loved how he felt until the Colonel and even then I didn't know he'd done that. He was sneaky about it."

I glance over to find her still looking up at the stars, so I continue. "Then going into the military and specifically the SEALs, I still wasn't surrounded with a bunch of dudes willing to pour their hearts out. There were several guys on my team who were married and although I felt like they all loved their wives, there were only one or two whom I ever heard say so out loud. It's just never been considered masculine to share feelings in any of the situations I've been in.

"It has recently been brought to my attention by more than one person that I need to start saying out loud what I'm feeling inside. Although I know the advice is good, it's still not easy. I don't think it'll ever be easy for me, but I refuse to lose you because I can't open my mouth. I hope you can be patient with me as I learn this new skill." She doesn't say anything. I'm not sure if it's because she's still mad or waiting to see if I'm finished.

Changing the subject for a moment I ask, "Can you believe how beautiful this sky is?"

"Wow," she breathes. "I think I can see a million stars all at once."

"I know. I used to do this when I lived here. I'd sneak out and drag a blanket to lie on so I could count the stars. I never thought there'd be anything more beautiful than the endless night sky, until I met you."

"Judson." She says it like she doesn't believe me so I roll to my side. She shifts her body and props her head in her hand as I mirror her action. "Quinn, it's not a line. It's the truth. Go back in time with me for a minute. It was your first day at pistol practice freshman year. You were coming through the doors from the locker room into the range. I was standing with the Colonel and

Chris Roberts. Your hair was shorter by a few inches and you had it in a ponytail. Your face was younger and makeup-free. I could see the hint of a silver chain tucked into the V of your shirt and the whole world stopped for me. Chris elbowed me in the gut when he caught me staring. I remember thinking I needed to be slapped, not elbowed, for having that reaction, considering I had Jenny back in Colorado waiting for me. But honestly, I couldn't take my eyes off you. I vowed then I'd never miss a practice if for no other reason than I wouldn't miss seeing you."

"Judson," she says it again, but I interrupt.

"I loved to hear your voice when you talked and your laughter made me happy. It bothered me when you stopped smiling and laughing. I wanted to kill the person that took that away from you.

"The night of the bathroom floor incident, I got home to the party and when I saw you going to the bedroom with that idiot Carl, I thought I'd kill him. I'd watched your downward spiral for months and knew something had happened, I just didn't think it was my place to approach you about it. So when it looked like you went to the bedroom with Carl willingly, I left you alone, fighting with myself not to go in after you. Not even 30 minutes later I could hear a commotion coming from the room and it wasn't the sound of good sex so I busted in and you were naked and getting sick. Carl was yelling and cussing. I was furious so I threw him out and the rest you know.

"What you don't know is every night after that, I wanted you more than the night before. I knew I could never have you. Jenny was my girl and I'm not a cheater so I relished the phone calls, the study sessions, the dinners, the laughs, the everything. The only thing that caused me hesitation when I signed up for the Navy was knowing I'd be leaving you in Ohio. Then I slept with you and second-guessed my decision to show up for boot camp all the way back to Colorado. I didn't want to leave you. I belonged to you, heart and soul, but I also knew you deserved better than me. The Navy was the right place for me at the time and I didn't want to leave you at home while I deployed for 9 to 18 months at a time. Especially since there was no guarantee I'd come home.

"One of the reasons I never wrote to you was because I knew you felt something for me too and I thought it would make things worse to keep in contact. I didn't want you to spend your days worrying about me. I wanted you to live and love and have a family and some stability. I've been with a lot of women since I left for the Navy, but I never spent more time with them than it took to get off. I never once thought of dating any of them, much less falling in love.

"My heart was already gone by the time I left. You owned it. You just didn't know it. That hasn't changed. What's changed is I'm finally willing to be selfish and beg you to be with me."

God, this is hard. I'm exhausted after spilling all of that but I hold her gaze. "Don't go back to Jeff. Stay with me, be patient with me, love me. I'm not sorry I fought with him today. I'd do it all over again if it meant he'd keep his paws off you. I love these," I trace the outline of her lips with my pointer finger, "and I don't want to share them." I thread my fingers into the hair on the side of her head and pull her to me. "Say you're mine, Quinn." A little whimper escapes her, but she says nothing. "Say it, Quinn." I tug on her hair as she groans, the sexy sound vibrates across my skin straight to my dick. "Quincy," I warn.

"I'm yours, Judson. Always yours."

I crush my mouth to hers. Our lips and tongues tangle in a frenzy of lust. It's messy and wild and hot as hell. So hot in fact that my dick is already hard. My body is responding to her like I'm a teenage boy with no control again. If I wasn't so damn happy to have normal function, I'd probably be embarrassed.

Showing her how I feel using my body seems like the most the important thing in the world to me right now. I press into her chest until she lies on her back. Then I push her shirt up above her bra and pull the cup under her heavy breast, pushing it up. I dip my head and suck the tip into my mouth and hum with contentment. Her back arches and her legs rub together restlessly. I pull the other cup down and repeat. "More, Judson, more," she breathes.

I give her what she wants, licking and sucking her sensitive flesh until she's panting so loud, so fast, I'm afraid she'll hyperventilate. First I drag her shirt off her body and then I slip the zipper of her jeans down and slide my hand into the small space under her panties, along her soft, bare flesh. Unable to move the way I want, I withdraw my hand and yank her jeans and panties off and set them aside. Her legs fall open and I slip two fingers into her wet heat. She squirms as I touch and rub her everywhere, avoiding direct contact with her clit. I want her begging for me, so I keep up the torture routine. It becomes obvious she's had enough when she pushes me to my back and straddles me, grinding against my jean-clad cock.

"Shirt off, handsome," she demands. I comply, yanking it off and tossing it to the side. When she leans down to kiss me, her hair falls like a black curtain around us and the smell of sweet citrus penetrates my nose. I've always loved the shampoo she uses. It takes me back in time to the last night I was in Ohio when I was finally able to lick, bite, touch and smell every inch of her skin. To when I was allowed to wrap her soft, thick hair around my fist and tug. She drags me back to the present with a playful nip of my lips as she grinds down again. I react the only way I know how. I grip her ass cheeks in my palms and flex up against her, signaling that I'm ready.

"I want you, Judson. Right here, right now."

"Take me then," I say with a smile I'm not sure she can see, but am certain she can feel against her lips. She shuffles my pants down over my hips and finds me commando. Before I can say anything else, her little hand wraps around my cock and she rubs the swollen crown around her hot, wet center, teasing me now. I groan impatiently until she impales herself with me. "Quinn!" I call out when we connect.

She pauses, flesh to flesh and I feel her muscles grip me inside like a vise. Her hips begin slowly with a gentle rocking motion, her body visible as a silhouette with the night sky as the backdrop. I swear, every teenage-boy fantasy I ever had out in this field is coming true right at this moment. When I was dating Jenny as a teenager, she was always too afraid of getting caught to try this.

I run my hands up over her hips, across her belly, over her rib cage and pinch the points of her breasts, still pushed up by the cups of her bra. She cries out as she increases her pace. I squeeze again and she changes direction, rolling her hips backward in a move that's got my mind flipping. Holy heaven, that's amazing!

"Don't stop, Daisy." Her pace stays the same as she continues to bend my brain with this move. "Quinn," I growl, unable to say anything else. I need more, faster, something.

She leans forward a little as she presses her hands to my chest for leverage, switching the motion altogether. She slides down slow at first, building momentum with each raise of her hips until she's moving fast and hard on me. I can tell when she's close as her pussy flutters around me and grips tighter like it's trying to pull me all the way inside her.

My back is digging into the grooves of my truck bed as she bounces down hard on me, but I don't care. I just want to make sure she doesn't stop. I'm close, but doing my best to hold out. Praying she'll get there quickly, I grip her hips tight, helping her to move faster. Her passionate moans fill the quiet night air until she belts out a scream that should bring the wildlife out to see what's going on. Her head rolls forward but she's still braced on me so I grip her hips again and pound up into her as hard as I can, ignoring the slight pain in my hip from the fight and the truck bed in my back. I concentrate on the feel of her wrapped around me tight.

"Holy shit, Daisy," I shout as I lift my hips and I release in her. I hold her hips flush to mine for a moment longer and pull her upper body down against me. We lie there waiting for our breath to return and I look at the stars, loving the fantasy I just lived out. The evening air might be cool but the heat between us is off the charts even as our bodies relax and recover.

The night is quiet except for the crickets who started singing again once we quieted down. "Are you going back to Denver, Quinn?"

Her head readjusts to rest her chin on her hands, which are laid out on my chest. If it were lighter out here I'd be able to see more than the outline of her head. Her hair is flowing over her and me, tickling my collarbone and rib cage as I wait for her response.

"I don't know what to do. I wasn't happy. I don't know if it was the culture in that particular unit I was assigned to or something I have to face as a police officer in general. I love being a cop, but it wasn't a welcoming environment for a woman, at least the department I was in."

"Whatever you do, I'll support it. I don't know what I want to do with the rest of my life. My plan changed when my body did and it's going to take me time to figure it out. I'm willing to go anywhere you go. I don't want to be away from you anymore. I know I'm an alcoholic and drug-addicted mess and it's going to take time for me to work through those issues, but I don't want to lose you in the process. I don't know how many more chances the universe is going to give me with you. I want to go where you go and work on being the man you deserve. I'm sorry I'm not already that guy."

Chapter Eleven

QUINN

I'M FLOORED. I didn't expect him to come back to the house ready to talk. I certainly didn't expect him to apologize or spill his guts. He's always been stoic. Always exemplified the strong silent type, even when he was dealing with my mess back in college. Not to say he doesn't talk at all, just not usually about feelings or emotional stuff. We always had good conversation though and he could make me laugh with his sarcastic, dry humor.

One thing has always been certain with him, if he cared about you, it was obvious, but in a subtle way. He didn't smother you with compliments or call you all the time or tell you how much he liked you, he just showed it.

With me, it was obvious in the crinkle of his eyes when we talked, the slight lift of his lips when he'd see me enter a room, the deep chuckle that seemed to come from all the way down in his shoes when he'd laugh at something I said or did. There were other times, when I was emotional, that his eyebrows would lower and pull together or he'd chew on the right side of his bottom lip as he listened to me. His friendship and concern were written right there in those tiny things that some people might overlook, but I never did. I made it my mission to study him and figure these things out.

He always kept eye contact during conversation and the biggest, most telling thing of all was when he approached someone or a group of people he liked. He sat down next to them to start conversation or he walked right up to join in. If you weren't someone he wanted to be around, he was cordial with a head nod to acknowledge you or he avoided you all together. He didn't back down from confrontation but he didn't seek it out either.

Judson must have been good at hiding his serious feelings down deep because I never suspected he was *in* to me. I was never sure why he took me in and took care of me. I guess I just thought he was a nice guy and after a while he realized we could really be friends. I also thought that his last night in Ohio, the first time we had sex, was based on his loneliness and the confusion of dealing with so many things at once.

The sex was so hot it was obvious we had chemistry, but it never occurred to me that he felt anything before that night and those particular circumstances. Sure, he said differently when we were in bed, but everyone knows when a guy is trying to get laid, he'll say anything.

As I lie here sprawled across his body, the cool breeze ruffles my hair, while his softening cock is still inside me as we talk. I'm wrapped comfortably tight in a peace I haven't felt in a long time.

"I don't want to leave Ms. Polly. I know she's a grown woman, but she has no family left and all of her friends are older. I want to be close enough so we can take care of her or help her if something happens. I put in an application with the Colorado Springs Police Department. They have a position open, but I'm not sure I'll get it. I'd like to find a house with a little land, maybe a small ranch where I can keep horses and stay in Colorado Springs, but all of that hinges on a job."

"You want horses and land?" I wish I could see the smile I hear in his voice.

"Well, yeah. Ugh, we haven't even talked about that."

My body tenses as I realize we haven't covered the subject of kids. He's known since college I couldn't have kids, but maybe he's like Jeff and thinks we can try some advanced technology or adopt or something.

"Hey, why did you tense up, Daisy?" he asks.

"I can't have babies. You know that, or maybe you forgot. You're still young and I'm sure you want them. Jeff wanted to see a specialist about new technology or use a surrogate, but I resigned myself a long time ago to no kids. I don't want them." I lay my head directly on his chest and listen to his heart for a few seconds, hoping this won't be the last I hear of it beating against my ear. No children could be a deal-breaker.

I feel him inhale before he says, "We never talked about exactly why you thought you couldn't have kids. You obviously never had a hysterectomy."

"When I miscarried that baby and almost bled out, the surgery to save me left too much scar tissue. My womb is now uninhabitable, kind of like Mars, according to the OB/GYN I saw a couple of months after the surgery."

"Well, it's not a problem for me. I've never been a baby person, I'd probably break one. Besides, I'm in no shape to be a parent. Never been able to see myself with a white-picket-fence-Ozzie-and-Harriet lifestyle. I'm okay sharing my life with just you. You're all I need." He wraps his arms around my back and holds me tight to his body while I melt into him, my mind settling on the new life I see slowly taking shape in my head.

Just to clarify, I ask, "Are you sure? I don't want us to start something and then in a couple of months you change your mind because I can't have kids. You have to be sure."

"Quince, I'm sure. You're all I need."

* * *

After a couple of months, we move Ms. Polly into a retirement community bungalow, the perfect size for her. She doesn't have to worry about lawn upkeep or snow shoveling, as it's all included in the community fees. Her house sold for the asking price so she was able to pay outright and have spending money left over. There's a clubhouse with activities every night and three of her close friends live in the same neighborhood.

Ready to start a new life, I resigned from my job in Denver and Judson and I bought a fixer-upper ranch on the outskirts of Colorado Springs. Seated on the plateau of a hill is a three bedroom, two bathroom single story house with an amazing stone fireplace on the main wall of the living room, an old barn behind the house, which needs a lot of work, and a beautiful pond on the backside of the property. The place is pretty run-down but Judson plans to do the work himself. He's decided this will be his project for now. Once it's finished he'll decide what career path he'll take. His disability check, along with my new paycheck from the Colorado Springs Police Department, pays our bills so we don't have to worry about financial issues. He's going to rebuild the barn first so we can board horses to bring in extra income too.

The land is amazing. It's 100 acres of varied terrain. It's good for hiking, horseback riding, fishing, hunting, and animal watching. Never in my life did I expect to own something this amazing. The day we closed on the property, Judson hung a sign on the front gate, christening the place Daisy Rivers Ranch. It's spectacular. My parents are coming to visit next month. My dad said he'll help Judson do some of the work and my mom plans to help me paint the inside of the house.

His mom lives about 20 minutes away and came to see the place with us on our second walk through. She loved it as much as we did. Although Joel, his brother, looked over the contracts for us, he hasn't said much. Judson said he's still mad about the addiction issues. We're hoping he gets over it soon because he has a seven-year-old son who loves to ride horses and we want to bring him here.

Judson may not want kids of his own, but he wants a relationship with his niece and nephew. Although his niece is only two and won't be riding horses for a while, he wants to see her, too. I'll give Joel time to come around before I go over there and light into him. Besides, we haven't bought horses yet. We want the barn to be safe before we add animals to the mix.

Life at the CSPD is great. The atmosphere here is much more laid back. That's not to say they don't take their jobs seriously, they do, but the approach is different.

I was pleasantly surprised during my first interview to find the chief of police here was on the national team with me my first year and remembered me as soon as he got my application. I think it helped me land the job. I've been assigned to the family crimes division, working with my partner on domestic violence and adult crimes. Seems like some of the worst of society can be found in the case files of this particular division.

Jasen Dexter, who prefers to be called Dex, is my partner. He's an enormous man built much like Judson, 6'4" and probably 230 pounds of solid muscle. He's a good guy, but quiet. We make a good team considering I'm comfortable with the quiet type. He joined the force several years ago when he returned from Afghanistan after serving six years in the Army.

I lie back against the cushions of our new couch and look at the vaulted, beamed ceiling for a few minutes before I turn my head to look at Judson, who's also looking at the ceiling. Our legs are splayed in front of us, heels to the coffee table, and by our limp postures it's obvious we're both tired.

"What are you thinking about, babe?" I ask as I reach for his hand, sliding my fingers between his.

"You. Us. This place," he answers as he squeezes my hand.

"Good or overwhelming?"

"Both. I'm happy. This is a good move for both of us. I'm happy we have our privacy together. I'm overwhelmed thinking about all I have to do around here, but at the same time, I'm content. I needed something to do and this is a good investment of my time and our money."

My heart warms with his words and his honesty. He's been working hard on sharing his feelings over the last six months. It's not been easy. When the anniversary of his accident came around, he was holed up in his room for two days and wouldn't talk to Ms. Polly or me. He missed counseling that week and I was afraid if he left the house we'd find him at the bar. He didn't leave though. He slept and did sit-ups and push-ups in his room for two days. He listened to music and read letters. He ate the food we left outside his door. We gave him his space but I was worried sick. Finally, at the end of the second day he crawled into bed with me and told me what was on his mind. His feelings were a mixed-up mess of relieved, sad, angry, happy, and confused. After those emotional days, he went back to working on improving his communication.

"I'm excited to see what you'll do with this place. I love the ideas you've sketched out. Tomorrow, let's unpack for a few hours and then walk down to the pond and fish for a little while. Well, you can fish and I'll sit out there with you and read." Fishing is not my thing.

"That sounds good. Come here," he pats his lap and I roll over to straddle his hips. He tugs on my ponytail as a lazy grin lifts one side of his mouth.

"I love you, Daisy."

"I love you, too."

His eyes survey my body, starting at the top of my head and moving slowly down, over my face, down my neck, over the curve of my breasts and down over my hips to the place where our bodies are joined. My hands rest on his chest as I note his nostrils flare and his pupils dilate. He slips one hand up the hem of my T-shirt and rubs his calloused fingers across my skin to the cotton of my bra. His pointer finger circles my nipple, bringing it to a sharp peak. He leans forward and nips at it with his teeth through the fabric. He knows this drives me wild. I whimper and push my chest forward in a silent request for more. His body jiggles with a chuckle. Bastard. It's obvious he loves the reaction he can draw out of me with minimal effort. If it didn't feel so good I'd stop him just to kill that arrogant gleam in his eyes.

"Now that we live alone, I can do this whenever I want," he explains with a wicked grin. I close my eyes and let my head lull back as he nips at my other nipple and licks it through my bra.

"It's been a long time since I could do this as slowly as I want to and put forth the right effort to get a vocal performance out of you. I usually have to hold back or cover your mouth to keep you quiet." He shakes his head, smile still in place. "Not anymore. Now you can scream the walls down for all I care." Excited by his words and ready to get this started, I roll my hips against his. The denim is a rough but welcomed friction against my most tender area.

"Stand up, Daisy."

I do as I'm told, knowing a reward is coming. He spreads his legs farther apart and pulls me in close between them. His palms grip my ass cheeks as he nuzzles my breasts. I want more. I need skin on skin. I need him inside me. I want to speed this up—I tend to get excited and rush—but I can't. I have to let him have control right now. He's in alpha mode and obviously getting off on having his orders followed.

I dig my fingers into the short hair on his head and scratch the way he likes it. I love the feel of the soft strands between my fingers.

He unbuttons my jeans and lowers the zipper at the slowest pace possible. I squirm, signaling I want him to speed up. He grips my hips to hold me in place, "Stop moving or we'll start all over."

"Babe, please," I whine. He loves when I beg and it's obvious, as the bulge in his jeans grows bigger. He wiggles his body a little and reaches between his legs to adjust himself with a groan.

Hooking his fingers in my jeans and panties, he lowers them to my knees. The denim is tight and holds my legs together. He slips one finger in between the damp folds and rubs across my clit, one, two, three times, with the perfect amount of pressure and it feels so good. He withdraws his fingers and lifts them to my lips. He likes it a little dirty so I close my mouth around the digits and taste the tang of my own arousal. I swirl my tongue around and suck hard. He groans again and pulls them out.

"Shimmy out of your jeans. Climb up here and straddle my face. I want to taste you." I feel the flush spread up my neck to my face. The ache between my legs grows with his naughty words so I do as I'm told and straddle his face, lifting one heel to the back of the couch. I'm afraid I'll suffocate him in this position if I don't. I can feel his breath across the exposed area and his fingers circle the opening twice smearing my juices up and over my clit.

"So damn wet, and I haven't even really started," he murmurs before he buries his face and strokes his tongue in and out of me, then up and over my pulsing clit.

"Judson," I squeak. My thighs are already trembling and he's barely gotten started. He can do this for 30 minutes at a time when he wants to torture me. It can be both heaven and hell all wrapped in one. I don't think I'll be able to hold my weight up in this position though if he drags this out. I'm usually flat on my back with my thighs spread as far as they'll go when he goes for the marathon munching session. Now I have to fight to stay conscious so I don't fall, which would be very unsexy, or collapse on his face and suffocate him. Also, unsexy.

"Relax, Daisy, I'm going to take my time. You're gonna come more than once this way so brace yourself."

"I can't. I'll fall. I need to lie down for this."

"No way. I've been dreaming of this for months while we waited to get our own place. I'm taking my time and getting this my way. Now brace yourself and let me get back to work."

I stifle a whimper by turning my head into my shoulder. He parts the lips of my sex with his fingers and laps at me like a kitten does milk. My legs are shaking bad now. He grips my hips hard and holds me in place while he sucks my clit into his mouth, flicking it with his tongue so many times I lose count and spiral into an explosive orgasm so big I forget where I am. I rock against him trying to ride it out.

Judson's chuckle vibrates the swollen flesh and triggers a second, smaller but still decipherable orgasm. I want to collapse. I want to lie down and take a nap, but I know I can't. He's determined. I have to endure more until he's had enough or decides he wants to fuck me more than eat me. After one more orgasm my legs give out and I slide awkwardly down his face and the side of his body in a heap, half straddling him and half balled up on the couch.

He smacks my ass hard enough I know there's going to be a handprint and demands, "Chest on the couch, ass in the air." I'm like a snail as I attempt to comply with his orders and my jellied body responds. When I'm up the way he wants me, he slaps my ass twice more and rubs the sting with his warm palm. I watch out of the corner of my eye as he studies his handiwork. He finally drops his pants and I realize he's been commando this whole time. About once a week he goes without boxers under his clothes and it turns me way the hell on. It's like he knows at some point he's going to fuck me and he wants to get to business quicker and easier. I crane my neck a little farther so I get a better look at him as he gives his cock a couple of fast pumps and rubs the swollen head against my soaked opening.

When he pushes inside until his hips are flush with my ass, a tortured moan escapes him and I squeeze my walls around him as tight as I can. He smacks my ass again. "Are you trying to make me come quick? If you keep that up it's going to happen."

I do it again to be naughty and wait for a slap that never comes. Instead I feel his knee slide up beside mine on the inside of the couch and his torso cover me. From the reflection I can now see in the window, we look like wild animals. His hips roll into mine, harder each time while the force of his thrusts scoot me down the couch. He bites into my shoulder and I cry out and push back against him. He does it again in a different spot and adjusts his angle, bucking harder each time. I'm screaming his name as he forces another orgasm out of me before I feel hot streams of fluid burst inside me and his weight collapse on me. The places he bit me are stinging a little, but the warm halo of post-orgasmic bliss is pulsing through me making it easier to ignore those. I need a nap.

"I think I'm going to like living alone with you even more than I thought," he comments, sounding out of breath.

I giggle and reply in the haughtiest voice I can muster, "I was kind of wondering if Ms. Polly would like a roommate. I don't think this is going to work for me."

"Really?" he asks as he pokes my ribs with his fingers, making my squeals ring out around the room. I'm ridiculously ticklish so I fight back, thrusting my hips, doing my best to dislodge him from his place on top of me. He continues to find those sensitive spots until I wiggle myself all the way to the floor, screaming and laughing all at once. I look up to where he's lying and find the biggest smile I've ever seen from him plastered across his face. The expression is so happy and relaxed it touches something deep inside me.

I sit up and brush my lips across his. "I love you, babe," I tell him. "Smile like that for me every day and I'll never leave." I trail my fingertips across his eyebrow and kiss him again.

"I'll do whatever it takes to keep you here every day, and if I wake up and you're by my side then it's likely you'll open your eyes to that smile," Judson remarks.

Chapter Twelve

QUINN

EVERY CITY HAS an area where the crime is higher than anywhere else and this is that neighborhood for Colorado Springs. I've been here several times a week since I started this job. So many times, in fact, that some of the faces on the street corners and porches are looking familiar. Dispatch is sending us to an apartment where there's been at least one other complaint since I completed my training a couple of months ago. The last time, it was for a domestic abuse situation and the neighbors called the cops when the yelling continued past 30 minutes and the woman's screams got too loud for the neighbor lady to hear the television. The victim was in bad enough shape she was admitted to the hospital and the perpetrator was thrown in jail. He didn't go down easy, but luckily he underestimated me and I was able to distract him while my partner dropped him. I can't imagine what the problem is today though because the guy, Howard Jackson, is still in jail and not supposed to get out until sometime next year at the earliest. His sentence is longer than normal because the domestic abuse was a parole violation.

I knock on the door and we wait. I'm standing in front because I can't see over Dex if he's in front. No answer, but I hear a loud thud on the wall near the door and a loud screech. I knock again, harder. "Open up, police!" I shout.

Inside, the yelling gets louder as something heavy sails through the glass window a foot to my right. My partner growls behind me and we both pull our weapons.

"Move over, Quinn," Dex commands.

I've learned not to argue with him so I step aside as he kicks the door with so much force it splinters into at least fifty pieces. He pushes through the jagged wood and steps inside. A groaning noise comes from the floor to my right and I look down to find the same victim from the last time, bloodied and beaten, lying on the floor. A bang sounds from the back room of the apartment and my partner takes off running in that direction while I call for an ambulance. He comes back a few minutes later, empty-handed and flaming pissed.

"What happened?" I ask.

"Bastard climbed out the window and took off down the fire escape. He was too far ahead of me. Did you call for a bus?"

"Yeah, they'll be here in less than five. Where's the boy?"

"Shit, I forgot about the kid. I didn't see him. Let's hope he's out somewhere. He didn't take the last beating too well."

Lateesha Brown is the victim's name and she's groaning, but not speaking. It's obvious her nose is broken by the odd direction the tip is facing. Blood covers her face and her jaw is swollen. I can't tell what else is wrong and I'm afraid to move her to check since I found her lying here. There's a good possibility of a head or neck injury. By the looks of her, this beating did more damage than the last.

Dex comes back into the room as the paramedics arrive. I give them the information I have on the woman and step back to speak with my partner. "What's up? The kid gone?"

"No, but he won't come out of the closet and I'm not dragging him out. I think we need to call in a social worker on this one. This kid has seen too much and with his dad in the clink and his mom headed to the hospital, I doubt he has anyone to take care of him."

"You call it in and I'll see what I can do to get him out of there."

I tiptoe into the room Dex indicated and step in front of the closet. The folding doors are wedged open and the kid, who's small for 10 years old, is squatting with his back against the closet wall, surrounded by old shoes and dirty clothes. His arms are wrapped around his knees and he's watching me like I'm a predator ready to attack him.

Carlo is half Hispanic and half African American with enormous brown eyes, a little round nose and full lips. His dark hair is coarse and kept short. The poor kid could blow away in a windstorm he's so skinny, but I suspect that's lack of effort from his mom when it comes to feeding the kid. The last time we were here I wanted to buy him a whole pizza when I saw his collarbones sticking out of his shirt.

"Carlo, come on out, buddy. You know I'm not going to hurt you. I was here before."

He shakes his head rapidly as a single tear trails down his caramel skin. I step in closer and squat down so I'm not looming over him. "Come on, Carlo, you know you can't stay here. I need you to come with me."

He shakes his head again.

"Okay, I get it. You're not ready. How about I sit here and keep you company until the social worker gets here?" I sit down and ignore the terrified bulging eyed look that crosses his face at the mention of the social worker.

"You don't like the social worker? I don't know who they're sending, but I'm sure it's someone nice. I haven't met a mean one yet."

His wide eyes lock on mine and for a brief moment I can see the pain this kid has already endured in his short life. This will be his third or fourth time in foster care and even though they were short stays I'm sure it was enough to stick with him.

"Carlo. No one is going to hurt you."

"It's not the social worker. It's the homes they stick me in, they're always bad," he whispers.

"What's bad about them, Carlo?"

He shakes his head.

"You can tell me. It's my job to keep you safe. If there's a problem I need to know about it."

More tears leak from his eyes and my heart twists uncomfortably. I wish he'd tell me what the issue is so I could fix it. Before I can ask any more questions, a homely woman, somewhere in her mid-fifties, with a fuzzy brown ponytail and ill-fitting clothes, pushes the door open and steps inside. She glances between Carlo and me and says, "I can take it from here, officer. I was a few buildings over when the call came in."

Carlo's tears fall heavier now and he crawls to get to me. As I stand he latches onto my waist with his bony little arms.

The social worker peels his fingers back, trying to make him let go. "She has to go back to work. You need to let her go. I'm going to take care of you." Her voice is flat like even she doesn't believe what she's saying and I have the most powerful urge to slap her hands away from him and hug him close to me.

I know it's an inappropriate response so instead I place a hand on her arm and say, "Give me a minute with him and he'll walk out of here with you, okay?" She stands, brushes her hands over her long frumpy skirt, stares at me for an uncomfortable minute, huffs out something under her breath and stomps out of the room.

I turn my attention to the sad little leach stuck to me. "Okay, here's the deal. You have to go with her, Carlo. It's the law. I'll find out where they placed you and come check on you tomorrow. I won't forget about you, okay? If you don't get up and walk out there, they'll drag you out and I don't want that to happen. Please, for me. I promise I'll see you tomorrow."

He holds tighter to me with his skinny little arms and I stroke the short, coarse hair on his head and say, "You have to trust me. I'm sure it's not easy for you. Just do what I ask." He lets go and slumps to the floor. I reach under his arms and pull him to a standing position. He stays on his feet and the defeat is obvious as he lowers his head and hunches his shoulders over. Finally, he takes the hand I offer to lead him out of the room.

The social worker is standing by the door talking to Dex when I appear. I lead Carlo over to her and say, "Carlo isn't going to give you any trouble, but I've promised I'll see him tomorrow wherever you place him."

"That's highly unusual, officer."

"Yes, I know. I don't make it a habit, but it's a deal he and I made and I'll hold up my end. I'll need the address and phone number of where he's going as soon as he's placed. I'll give you my number and you can call or text it to me later today. If I don't hear from you I'll track you down tomorrow."

Her face is tomato red. She's pissed, but I don't care. I'm not trying to check up on her, I'm trying to make sure a scared, neglected kid is made to feel comfortable. If it takes some extra effort on my part, so be it. "I'm not trying to step on your toes. I just want to make this easier for him."

She nods once and taps him on the shoulder. "Let's go. I'll get the officer your foster home information so she can see you." She snatches her purse off the floor and pulls him behind her. His wide eyes watch me until he disappears around the corner.

* * *

"How was your day?" Judson asks as he sets a plate down in front of me with a juicy steak and a large, steaming baked potato. His clothes are dingy from working in the barn all day, but his expression is light, like he feels good about what he's doing with his time.

"Rough. Dex and I broke up a nasty domestic dispute between an adult brother and sister. The sister was in bad shape. We found her 10-year-old kid crouched in the closet amongst a pile of dirty clothes and shoes, hiding. We've been to that place before, when she got beat up by her boyfriend. Poor kid's seen way too much for his age. He latched onto me and didn't want to let go. I hate that part of the job. The social worker showed up and it was obvious she didn't give a shit what happened to him. She's working only for the paycheck. I know her job is difficult, but that kid could've used a soft touch after everything he's been through. I had to promise to drop by and see him tomorrow at his foster home."

Judson doesn't respond. He must realize nothing he says will shovel the shit out of this day. He reaches across the table and covers my hand with his. I look up and notice the tender expression he's giving me and I'm taken back to the night on the bathroom floor when he gave me a similar look.

The emotion of the day finally overflows and my eyes fill with tears. I tend to be pretty tough but when it comes to kids I crumble. Judson pushes his chair back and pats his lap. I don't hesitate. I move around the table and straddle his lap. He pulls my head to his shoulder and rubs soft comforting circles around my back. I feel sweet kisses every so often on my hair as I cry.

"I'm supposed to be a tough cop, not a crying girly girl," I whine.

"You're supposed to be you. It's what makes you good at your job. If that didn't affect you, I'd be more worried for you than I am about your crying. Compassion is what separates you from so many others. It's okay. No one has to know other than me."

"Thank you," I tell him, my voice barely a whisper.

He carries me to the bedroom, leaving our lovely meal uneaten and strips off my clothes. I stand there as he retreats to the bathroom. I can hear the water flowing in our oversized claw-footed bathtub. When he returns, he takes his own clothes off and leads me to the bathroom. He sits on the edge of the tub and removes his prosthesis, then lowers himself into the tub before reaching his hand out for me. I sit down in between his legs and rest against him. He grabs the bath gel to squirt in his hands, rubs them together and washes me all over. My nipples are tight little peaks by the time he finishes.

Judson has officially taken my mind off of things as he teases me by skirting close but not touching my most sensitive places. I know he's distracting me from my long day with the hint of sex and I'm so thankful we live alone together now.

As his hands drift down my chest again, I arch up and out, trying to get direct contact with his fingers. He chuckles and slips down the sides, lifting the weight of each breast but steering clear of the nipple.

"Please, touch me," I beg. His lips brush my neck and lead up to my ear where he circles the lobe with his tongue.

"Shhh. Be patient," he tells me. *Why does he have so much patience when I'm a wild bundle of need and want?* Goose bumps spread across my skin while his hands slide down under the water where I open my legs, welcoming him.

"So greedy, Daisy," he murmurs in my ear. Both hands sweep over my thighs and push them further open. "So beautiful. So perfect." His fingers trail from my knee to the apex of my thighs and separate the lips of my sex. I squirm as he plays this game of teasing me. He's close to where I want him but not quite there and the sound of my increased breathing seems loud enough to echo around the room. His fingers circle the opening and rub up, trapping my clit as they slide past the swollen flesh. I mew and press my hips up against his fingers.

"Patience. I'm taking my time." His voice seems like more of a growl.

"No, no patience. I need you now."

His teeth nip at my earlobe. "I said be patient," he commands. Both hands slide over my belly, up my rib cage and palm the weight of my breasts again. His thumb and forefinger pinch and twist my nipples and I feel desire zing through me straight to my center.

"Judson," I call out, "more!" He pinches and twists harder this time and I lower my hand to between my legs and circle, unable to wait any longer. If he won't take care of me, I'll take care of myself. I make four or five circles over my throbbing clit before his hand captures my wrist. "No, Daisy, this is my job. Just hold still. I promise to reward good behavior."

"I can't wait. I need it." *When did I start sounding this whiney?*

"Yeah, you can."

His erection is rock-hard against my back and I hope he won't be able to hold out much longer. He keeps one hand on my breast, pinching and plucking, while the other disappears between my legs. One thick finger pushes inside me with ease and I squeeze around it. He slides it in and out a few times and then adds a second finger. Knowing he's not going to increase the pace, I let my head lull back against his chest and turn it to the side. When I open my eyes his nipple is right there within my reach so I flick it with my tongue and he tenses.

"What are you doing, Daisy?"

I don't answer. I swipe at it again. He flexes into my back. Now that I'm certain he likes it, I turn my face more fully into him and suck it into my mouth, trapping it with my teeth.

"Quinn," he groans, his voice deeper with lust. I can't help the smile that spreads across my face at his reaction and I lose the beaded tip. I lean in and repeat the process and his fingers fuck me harder. His control is slipping with each pull of my lips.

He removes his hand altogether and flattens it against my pussy.

"Stop," he demands. I lean back and still myself, waiting for him to tell me what he wants. I'm pretty sure I'm about to get what I want. He pulls in a deep breath and says, "Sit up and turn. I want you on my dick and I want to watch your face as you take it. I scramble to comply, sending water splashing over the sides in my excitement. As he straightens both legs, he palms his cock, stroking while he watches me get into position like he asked. It's a tight fit in this tub and it doesn't help that he's a big guy and takes up a lot of space. With both my knees trapped on the outside of his hips I lower myself onto him. He aligns us and I drop all the way down. My head flies back and I release a whimper of delight. He grips the cheeks of my ass and lifts to start my movement. I follow his lead. My breasts bounce between us and I watch as he licks his lips in response. He continues to guide my hips but lowers his head in an attempt to capture a nipple. I release the side of the tub I was using for leverage and hold my breast in my hand, guiding it to his mouth. He tugs at the tip, elongating the pink flesh before flicking it with his wicked tongue.

I switch breasts and offer up the other, wanting to balance the sensation. His tongue swipes at me and I press it closer to his face. He nips harder this time and he flexes up into me as I drop down. My eyes widen at the fuller, deeper sensation while his lips form a naughty smirk.

With a tighter grip on my hips, he powers up, switching the pace to high. Water is sloshing all over the bathroom as we fumble through with lack of leverage and slippery ceramic, but I ignore what's certain to be a big mess. Instead, I concentrate on the buzzing at my core. It's signaling that I'm close to a powerful eruption, one that's sure to consume me. I adjust so I'm on my feet crouched over him. The burn in my thighs is holding back the orgasm that looms so close, but I don't let it stop me from moving.

When his eyes shift from the place our bodies are joined and lock on mine, I see lust, need, excitement, tension, and love all twisting together until he presses his finger to my clit and swirls a couple of times. Then my eyes close as my orgasm takes me to the far reaches of outer space. He grips tighter and thrusts two more times until his cock expands and explodes deep inside me. His head falls back against the tub with a thud and I lean forward so I'm close enough to reach behind him to feel if he did any physical damage.

He wraps his fingers around my wrist and pulls it to his lips. "I'm okay, Daisy. Come here."

I lie against his chest while our bodies settle. Most of the water is out of the tub and the cool air settles over my heated skin, chilling it slightly.

"Thanks for making a crappy day better. I love you."

"Me too. I probably should have tried talking to you instead of fucking you till you forget about your shitty day though. That was my intention when we came in here but as soon as you pressed up against me I couldn't remember my plan. I'm sorry. Please be patient with me."

"You're not going to get any complaints from me. I like how you handled that situation. As far as everything else, I think you're doing well. Do I want you to tell me what you're feeling? Yes, but I also know it takes time. It's only been six months since you started therapy. Give yourself some credit. Besides, I don't want to change you, just make life better for you."

He kisses the top of my head and holds me close until the remaining water cools too much to stay in. Then we get out and he cleans up the flooded mess while I nuke our dinner in the microwave. Afterwards he carries me to bed where we lie for another hour as I listen to him talk about all the progress he made to the barn today.

* * *

It's noon when Dex and I finally finish all the paperwork piled up in our inboxes. There have been no callouts so far today so we're going to the social worker's office. I'm amazed she's there when we arrive. There are stacks of papers covering all of her desk except the area her computer is on and she looks exhausted.

"Officers," she greets us. It's obvious she's not happy to see us, but I don't care. It's not that I want to make things hard for her, but my concern is Carlo, not if I'm interrupting her paperwork time.

"Ms. Winsted. Sorry to bother you. I'd like the address to the home Carlo is staying in. I'll make the visit after school."

Her sigh is heavy as she replies, "You can go now. He didn't go to school today. There was a scuffle at the house last night and the housemother decided Carlo should stay home and acclimate to his new surroundings."

"What do you mean a scuffle?" I narrow my eyes on her.

She huffs. "He got into a fight with another boy right before bedtime last night."

I take a step forward, my anger rising at the flippant way she shares the information. Dex grabs my arm and gives it a warning squeeze. I stop moving but keep my eyes trained on her, waiting for a response.

"I'm not sure what the circumstances were, but it was an older kid he fought with. He got beat up and wasn't in any shape to go to school today. He's okay, officer. He's used to this kind of thing and it was his mouth that got him in trouble in the first place."

"He's 10 years old. What do you mean he's used to this and *his* mouth got him into this?" My voice rises a few octaves when Dex clears his throat and pulls me flush against him.

"I *mean*, officer, this is not uncommon in the foster care system, especially with the group homes. There's a pecking order amongst the kids and he stepped out of line. I'm not condoning the behavior but I'm telling you it could have been avoided if he wanted it to be. The other boy has been punished. I have to get back to work, here's the address," she scribbles it on a piece of paper and hands it to me. "It's not as bad as it looks. I'll check on him later. I'm buried in cases here. There are 100 more kids in my caseload who need follow-ups and I have to get all this paperwork done."

I look at everything on her desk and realize she's drowning in paperwork and issues and probably even the kids themselves. There obviously aren't enough people in this department and she's doing the best she can. Even though it's not close to good enough, there's nothing I can say to make her feel worse than she already does.

"Thank you for the address, Ms. Winsted. We'll make the visit now." She nods and returns to her paperwork.

Twenty minutes later we pull up to a large two-story house at the back of a suburban neighborhood. It's a little run-down with peeling baby blue paint and unattended flowerbeds. Bikes and various toys litter the yard, leaving no question that children live here. We ring the doorbell and an older woman answers. She's wearing spandex pants meant for someone half her age and size, and a short long-sleeved T-shirt that barely covers her waist. It's not an attractive look.

"Can I help you, officers?"

"Yes, we're here to see Carlo Brown."

She squints her eyes. "Why?"

"We were there when he was removed from his home yesterday and promised to check on him. The social worker said he'd be home today acclimating after an issue last night."

"Yeah, he's here. Follow me." She turns without so much as a smile and saunters through the house, down the stairs to the basement as we trail along. The basement is divided off into three sections, each with two twin beds. There are three dressers and one closet. The lighting is dim, but sufficient, and the air is damp and cool. I'm wondering if they bring in space heaters at night to help keep the kids warm. It's winter and basements can get very cold.

On a twin bed pushed against the far wall is Carlo. His back is against the wall and his bottom on the mattress. His arms are wrapped around his knees with his cheek resting on top facing the other direction.

"Carlo?" I call to him and his eyes lift slowly. I'm struck in an instant by the look of defeat on his little face. I'm also enraged in the same instant by the condition his face is in. His eye is swollen almost shut and his lip is busted. The beautiful caramel skin of his cheek is marred by the four, deep, red scratches running down toward his neck. I can't help the gasp that flies out. Dex places a hand on my shoulder as if telling me to get it together without actually saying the words.

"Carlo. It's Officer Hannigan and Officer Dexter, from yesterday. I promised I'd come by to see you. How are you feeling?" I approach like I'm dealing with a wounded, cornered animal. He continues his silence. His eyes flick to the foster mother and back to me as he remains mute.

"Carlo, can you explain what happened to you?"

The foster mother clears her throat and Carlo's eyes flick to her again and back to me. He shakes his head and looks down at his knees.

I turn to the woman and say, "I'd like you to give us a few minutes alone with him."

"That's not normal, officer." She stands defensively with her arms crossed over her chest, hip popped out like she's an irritated teenager.

I can feel the growl building up inside me because I know she's covering up something here, but I don't get a chance to say a word. Dex turns to her with his best shut-up-or-suffer face and says, "I don't care how irregular it is. We're officers of the law and are requesting a moment with this young man to hear from his mouth why he looks like he was in a cage match since we saw him yesterday afternoon. We can do it this way or I can call the social worker and request a full investigation." His expression is stony as he faces off with her.

She stares at Carlo, never blinking, never breaking eye

contact, like she's trying to convey something silently. Then she spins on her heel and stomps back up the stairs. I release the breath I'd been holding and sit on the edge of the bed.

"Carlo, look at me." His big doe eyes, so sad, meet mine and I know whatever he faced here is bad. "I can't help you if you don't tell me what happened. I need to know everything."

He lays his head back on his knees, looking away from us and says, "Nothing. It was nothing." He won't look at either of us and he won't say anything else.

"Carlo, please tell us. If not, I'll call the social worker and tell her you need a visit now."

"It won't matter. She'll leave me here and then I'll be in trouble for having her come here. Just leave it alone." He sounds defeated, like he's done this dance before and knows the outcome.

Dex finally sits down and shares, "Listen, kid, I grew up in the system and I'm not leaving this damn house until you tell me what happened. I know the code. You never rat on anyone, but I can't leave you here looking like that since I have an idea how it happened. Start talking. Once I know the story we'll decide how to proceed, but I'm finding out the story one way or another." Carlo stares at him for what feels like an eternity but is really only a couple of minutes. I don't move a muscle, afraid I'll end the standoff.

"This kid, Jeremy, he's tough. He wanted to make sure I know whose house this is. He ain't got no patience for new kids. Didn't want me to get any ideas about being a favorite with the foster parents. He picked the fight and blamed it on me. Then all the kids backed him up because they are scared to go against him. I'll be fine. If you make a big deal they'll punish me more. Even the foster parents."

Dex swears under his breath and stands to pace the room. "Let me think," he says. Carlo and I watch him go back and forth for five full minutes, not saying a word. Finally, Dex stops and asks, "You unpacked yet?"

Carlo nods.

"Okay, then grab what little you brought with you. You're coming with us. I'm not leaving you here to deal with Jeremy or the foster parents." Dex looks at me. "Call the social worker and tell her we're on our way to her office and she needs to be prepared to place him somewhere else. We can explain when we get there. Don't let her give you any lip. I'm not messing around with this shit. Someone should have been out here to document this. No kid should have to worry about this in his home, foster care of otherwise." He shifts his focus to Carlo. "Grab your stuff and we'll carry it out of here. Where's your coat? It's really cold outside. Probably going to snow later today."

"I ain't got one. I only got a few things."

"No coat," Dex huffs under his breath. I've seen Dex irritated but never pissed like this.

Carlo crawls off the bed and winces as he twists his torso.

"Stop," I demand. He looks at me with weary eyes. "Why are you moving around awkwardly?"

"I got hit in the side. It's nothin'."

Dex doesn't even blink. He strides over and lifts the side of Carlo's shirt. There's a purple and red bruise the size of a giant Denny's pancake on his side, half on his ribs and half off. Dex swears and I feel the burn of tears at the back of my eyes. *What went on here last night?*

I blink them back and tell him, "Okay, get your stuff. I'm going to step outside and call Ms. Winsted and have a word with the foster mother. It's going to be okay."

Bounding up the stairs, my anger boils inside like seafood at a low country boil. I find the foster mother. "I'm calling the social worker now. We're removing Carlo from the home. He's in worse shape than we were led to believe. You'd better hope you filed the proper forms for this or you'll have to answer for more than just what's happened to him. I'm sure this isn't the first incident in this house."

The terrified expression on her face tells me she didn't do anything except tell the social worker there was a fight. She was going to push this under the rug and hope it went away. I wonder how many other kids have suffered at Jeremy's hands and nothing has been done. Footsteps clump in behind me and Carlo slides up beside me. I place a gentle hand on his head.

"Come here and let her see the bruise on your side." His eyes echo the fear of earlier. "It's okay, buddy. Just show her."

He lifts his shirt and the moment the full thing comes into view she gasps and slaps a hand to her mouth. She shakes her head in a quick jerky motion. "I didn't know it was there. I didn't know."

I push Carlo behind me protectively and say through clenched teeth, "That's probably true, but you knew his eye is swollen shut, his lip is busted and he has bear claw type scratches down his face. He should've had a full exam after the fight, just by looking at his eye. He can barely open the damn thing. I'm not sure what punishment you gave Jeremy, but I'm not sure it was enough It's now become my mission to see that someone will handle this properly. This kid was taken away from his mother yesterday and placed in a strange home with people he doesn't know, and instead of trying to help him get acclimated you let him get the shit beat out of him. I'm not okay with it and neither is my partner. He happens to be a product of the system so he knows how this goes. Nothing gets by him so I'm thinking you might be a little screwed." I turn to Dex and instruct, "Go load him up while I call."

Before he leads Carlo out the door he removes his coat and drapes the giant piece of clothing over him. "It's too cold to take him out without a coat. He can use mine and I'll get him one on the way to the social worker's office." He points at the foster mother and says, "That should have already been taken care of.

If he didn't get beat up, he'd be at school right now with no coat."

The foster mother says nothing.

I call the social worker, who seems more bored than concerned, to inform her of the fact that we've pulled him from the home. By the time I get to the car I'm seething mad. Doesn't anyone care what happens to Carlo? No wonder he was hiding in the closet when we came for him. I'm surprised he didn't jump out the window and run.

* * *

When I shuffle through the door of our home at the end of my shift, I find the table set with candlelight and soft music playing in the background. Judson's in the kitchen in a well-worn T-shirt, threadbare blue jeans, and shoeless. His short hair is damp and a little messy, like he didn't comb it after his shower, and the five o'clock shadow I left him with in bed this morning is a little heavier, almost making a full beard. A kitchen towel is thrown haphazardly over one shoulder and a spatula is in his hand. His smile is bright against his dark facial hair and the little crinkles in the corners of his eyes give his sexy smile even more character. A little bit of my shitty day fades away as he greets me with a kiss that would melt the panties off a Victoria's Secret model. "Hey, Daisy, how was your day?"

I sigh and drag off my coat, hanging it on the coatrack by the door. "Shitty. It was horrible. Carlo, that kid I told you about yesterday, he got beat up pretty bad at the foster home. I'm glad we checked on him because the foster parents were acting like nothing happened. We pulled him from the home and had him placed with an elderly couple who only take on special cases. Dex is pissed. He's made this kid a priority and we'll make sure he gets taken care of."

Judson squints as he studies me for a second. "Are you okay?"

I shrug. "I'm not happy about any of it. You should've seen him. He looked like he'd been in an MMA fight. He's 10 freakin' years old. He should be protected, not used as a punching bag."

"I'm sorry your day was bad. I'll do my best to make it better. Go get changed. Dinner will be on the table when you get back, then I'm taking you to see something amazing."

He looks like a little kid as he smiles at me, anxious to share something new.

"Okay, I'll be back out in a few minutes." He brushes his lips against mine and turns back to the kitchen. It's then I notice his pronounced limp, which only happens when his body is tired or he's pushed himself too hard physically. I don't say a word. I figure I'll ask questions at dinner.

Chapter Thirteen

QUINN

A COUPLE of lovely hours later we are in the truck, bumping down the dirt road towards the pond. The snow flurries are floating down and melting to water droplets the instant they hit the warm windshield. It looks like something out of a movie filled with magical creatures and snowy meadows. He pulls up to the parking spot he cleared out when we first moved in, turns around and backs in. Once the keys are out of the ignition he says, "Come on, meet me around back." I do as I'm told and when I reach the tailgate of the truck he's spreading a heavy blanket across the bed. "Climb up here, Daisy." He wiggles his gloved fingers at me and helps me to sit on the edge of the tailgate. "Let your eyes get acclimated to the dark."

"Isn't it a little cold to hang out in the back of your truck tonight?" I don't normally question him, but it's cold, I'm tired and it's already been a long day.

His left cheek ticks up on the side with a half grin. "It'll be worth it. I know after the day you had, you need some peace and this is as peaceful as it gets. Now scoot back and lie down facing the sky."

I do as I'm told and I feel the truck shake with the weight of his body adjustment. He covers me with an extra blanket and settles next to me. Our shoulders are touching and we're both on our backs. I can feel cold little flakes landing on the exposed skin of my face. The air around us is silent, the way it gets when the snow is floating from the sky like it has all the time in the world to reach the ground. The wind isn't even blowing tonight. The faint hint of Judson's cologne and the evergreen scent from the pines all over the property permeate the air. I take a deep breath and soak it in. As I'm letting it out, a beam of light shines into the sky next to me. It's a high-powered flashlight and it's illuminating the snowflakes as they make their way down to cover us. It's amazing. I've never seen anything like it. I grew up with snow in the winter but have never done this before.

"Wow," I whisper, afraid to be too loud and corrupt the peacefulness of the moment.

"I knew you'd like it. My brother and I used to ride out to the field, away from the lights of the house and barn to do this. We always thought it was so cool. I wonder if he's shown his kids this trick yet. Mom showed us this. She said it was like being in our own snow globe."

"She's right! It's like magic. I love it. Thank you."

After 10 minutes he passes me the flashlight and turns to his side. I adjust the beam so it's aimed just right.

"I love you more than anything, Quinn. I've been doing a lot of thinking and I realize I wasn't the softest guy in the world before the Navy, but I was better at all of this relationship stuff and some days I wish I was still the man I was our last night in Columbus together."

"I don't. I don't want you any way but how you are right now. I want you to open up to me a little more, but I'm not disappointed in you, physically or emotionally. I love every part of you. I'm proud to have a warrior at my side." He leans down and presses his cold lips to mine and for a moment I forget I'm lying in the back of his truck in the freezing weather as the snow falls all around us. I'm just a girl, in love with a boy, in a moment I wouldn't trade for anything.

"I'm going to spend the rest of my life showing you how much I love you. So you'll know I realize what I have with you is priceless and perfect."

"Judson," I whisper, a little sad at his declaration. Even though I have Judson, I still don't see the point in getting married. I don't want to trap him with me in case he decides he does want kids. It'll be easier for him to leave if it ever comes to that.

Almost like he can read my mind he says, "Quinn, we don't have to get married to be together forever. We just have to love each other and fight through the hard times together." He kisses me breathless and then rolls to his back, taking the flashlight again. We lie there in silence for another half hour, enjoying our life-size snow globe as the peace consumes us both.

On the ride back to the house I ask, "Did you really mean it when you said I could ask you anything?" I chew the side of my lip. It makes me nervous to ask him certain questions but I'm anxious to hear the answers.

"Of course," he replies, his eyes still on the road.

"Since you ended up back in your hometown, are you sorry you gave up Jenny and the chance at a family?"

He stops the truck right in the middle of the dirt road, throws it in park and rests his hands in his lap. The light from the dashboard illuminates his face enough I can see the strain in his eyes.

He doesn't hesitate to give me his answer. "No, I'm not. I needed to see the world and serve my country. I needed the escape and the challenge that the SEALs provided."

"What about Jenny?" I ask in a quiet voice. He turns to face me and reaches across the space of the cab. "I was in love with you before I broke up with Jenny. I told you that. I know it's wrong, even now I feel bad about it, but it's the truth. I was never meant to be with Jenny. I should have broken up with her the day after I woke up with you on my bathroom floor. I love you, I have for a long time, but I was such an emotional mess and going into a dangerous profession. I didn't think it was fair to drag you into the military life. I wanted you to have a normal life with a husband who'd be home every night to love you and take care of you."

I turn away as I confess, "I saw you with her on the porch during your recovery. It made me wonder if you wish there had been more. If you wish you made different choices. She's still beautiful."

"Why didn't you tell me you were jealous all this time?" he teases me, his tone different from a moment ago. I keep my eyes turned away so he can't see what's brewing in them.

"Hey. Look at me, Quincy." I hesitate before I turn to face him. "I love you. You aren't my consolation prize because Jenny didn't wait for me. You are the prize. She even told me that day on the back porch that she thought we, you and I, belong together. Even she knows. I don't need a family, other than you. If you don't want to get married we won't, but you're still mine. Always will be. Don't ever doubt it."

JUDSON

Three months have passed since we bought this property and I can't help but be proud of the finished barn, which is now safe and functional. Every piece of rotting wood has been replaced and the whole thing has been painted on the outside. The finished product is a big red barn like something you might find in a children's picture book.

I have a man named Connor coming by to check out the property and discuss fees. He bought a horse for his daughter and needs to board him somewhere. I'm hoping he chooses us so we'll have some income to help us afford more of the renovations we want to make on the house and the landscaping in the spring. I'd love to surprise Quinn with the news.

A heavy-duty black pickup truck pulls into the driveway and parks. A tall, middle-aged man wearing a tan cowboy hat, jeans, a flannel shirt, and boots hops out of the truck and rounds the hood. I step through the gate and leave it open behind me. We shake hands and I introduce myself and usher him towards the barn.

"Connor, I just replaced all of the beams and updated the equipment. We have a pond on the back part of the property and plenty of trails to take the horses on. Our plan is to add some help after we get a few horses, but for now I'll be handling the care. My lady is a police officer on shift work, but she'll help when she's here. I grew up around here and raised horses on a farm with my family so I know all that's needed. We have a friend who's a large animal vet and willing to make house calls for us if need be. If we plan to leave town for any reason, I've got someone I trust willing to stay while we're gone."

He looks me over once with a thoughtful expression and finally says, "I'm not trying to be an asshole, but I have to ask if you're physically up for this task. I'm not sure what caused that..." he gestures to my prosthesis, which is only visible at the foot and ankle right now, and continues, "but I don't want to go to all the trouble of paperwork and insurance and transport if this is doomed from the start."

I stand up straighter for a second and mull over what he's just said. "Sir, I'm a former Navy SEAL, had this happen while on patrol in Afghanistan almost two years ago. Although it looks bad I can assure you I'm in top physical condition. I did all of the renovations on this place myself. I only had help with things requiring two sets of hands. I work out every day and can probably handle more physical exertion than you can with both legs, to be quite honest. I understand if your concern keeps you from boarding your horse here, but I think you're making a mistake. The attention your horse will get here will have no comparison at other stables." I keep my shoulders squared and my eyes locked on his. I understand his worry, but there's no way I'll buckle under that kind of scrutiny. I've fought long and hard to get back in shape, both physically and mentally.

There's a long pause while Connor studies me, eyes squinted in thought.

"Afghanistan?"

"Yeah."

"I served in Desert Storm. I was Army, but I get it. I'm sure you're right by saying our horse will get more attention here so we'll try it out. I can deliver him this weekend if that works for you."

"That's fine. We can fill out the paperwork when you drop off. You'll be able to meet Quinn at that time too, she's off this weekend."

He shakes my hand and smiles at me. "Good doin' business with you, man."

When he pulls out of the driveway I breathe a sigh of relief and grin, knowing all of my hard work on that barn is about to pay off.

Two hours later, Quinn pulls up. I remove the chicken breasts from the grill and place them on a plate as she makes her way up the porch stairs and through the door.

"Hey, Daisy," I say as I kiss her forehead.

She peers up at me through her long dark lashes and asks, "Isn't it a little cold out here to be grilling?"

"It's never too cold to grill. I was bored with the oven so I decided to try something different. How was work today?"

"Long. I did see Carlo and his mom today. They're both going to counseling now and we're hoping she's done dealing with assholes. Her brother will be in jail for another couple weeks but they have a restraining order on him to keep him away once he's out."

Carlo has been a concern of Quinn's since the day she met

him, but after he got beat up in the foster home the last time she's taken a special interest in him.

"Good. I'm glad his family is on the mend. By the way, Saturday morning, we're getting our first boarder." Surprise flashes across her face right before she jumps up and down squealing.

* * *

Three weeks after we took on the first horse, we got another one, on a recommendation from Connor. I've been out on the trail with the new horse for an hour when my cell phone rings.

"Hey, Daisy."

"Hey, babe. Bad news, I'm going to be late."

"You alright?"

"Yes, no. Not really. We just left Carlo's mom's house. She's at the hospital and is being taken into surgery. Her brother broke the restraining order and beat her pretty bad. I'm not sure if she's going to make it this time." The sadness in her voice is so heavy I can almost feel it through the phone.

"How's he doing?" I ask, knowing the answer is not going to be great, but still needing to hear it. I haven't met the kid, but I know Quinn adores him and has made a point to stay active in his life since she met him. Dex even has a soft spot for the kid and as far as I can tell, the man doesn't have a soft spot for humans in general. Animals, yes. Humans, no.

"It's bad. He tried to jump in and help her, but got thrown against the wall and knocked out cold. When he came to, the uncle was gone and his mom was beaten so bad she was unrecognizable and unconscious. He called Dex directly, not even 911. Dex is with him right now. We're trying to get him placed with the older couple who took him last time. The social worker and I are about to go head to head if she doesn't get her head out of her ass and realize we aren't going away until she does the absolute best she can with this situation."

"I'm sorry. Just call and let me know what time you're headed this way and I'll have dinner ready."

"It may be a while, but I'll call. I love you."

"Love you, too." Without a goodbye, she hangs up. I take Comet, the new horse, into the barn and brush him down. The whole time I work I can think of nothing but Carlo and his mother and what their life must be like.

By the time Quinn gets home it's 10 o'clock and I can tell by the look on her face her nerves are frayed. She's a pretty calm woman most of the time so tonight must have been bad.

"You okay?" I ask as I wrap my arms around her.

"No," she grumbles into my neck as she holds me tight around the waist.

"Come on and eat and tell me everything."

I lead her to the table and pull out her chair. I serve her dinner and sit patiently, waiting for her to tell me.

"The older couple couldn't take Carlo this time. The husband just had surgery and they're off the list for a while. He almost ended up at the home where he got the beat down, but Dex flipped out and had him placed in a different group home. This time we accompanied him there and Dex made it known they'd deal with him if Carlo wasn't taken care of properly. It was stressful. I know I'm going to have a hard time sleeping just thinking about him. The poor kid has been through so much and now they aren't sure if his mom's going to survive. She just got her life turned around and was doing better. I thought they actually had a future on the right side of the law."

We spend the next hour talking about her work and the horses until she finally falls asleep on the couch as I rub her feet. I carry her to our room, help her undress, lay her under the covers and slip in behind her. For hours I hold her, thinking of ways to make things easier for her.

* * *

At breakfast the next morning, I say, "I thought about it for a long time after you went to sleep and I think we should become foster parents." I hold my breath waiting for her response. Knowing she never wants kids had me nervous to bring this up, but it feels like the right thing.

Her fork lowers from her mouth slowly. She wipes her lips with her napkin and asks, "What are you talking about?"

"Listen, just...listen. Don't say anything until I'm done, okay?"

She nods so I continue.

"We have two extra rooms in the house. I'm here almost 24/7. We have plenty of area for kids to play. They could help with the horses if they want and they'd be safe here. I'm not sure what hoops we'd have to jump through, but I think it'd be worth it. Then when you have a kid like Carlo who needs somewhere to stay, he can come here. We aren't having any of our own kids, and believe me I'm okay with that, but we can make a difference, together. I know you don't want kids at all, but in this scenario it's not a permanent thing, kids would come and kids would go. We could start out just having one and see how it works out. If we don't like it, we can stop. If you don't like the idea, I won't bring it up again, I just thought it might be cool. I know it won't always be easy, but it'll be worth it. Just think about it."

She looks at me for a long moment and finally says, "Let me think about it. I don't know if they'll consider us."

"No one's perfect. However, you're a police officer and I'm a highly decorated combat veteran who's still in touch with a counselor. We have a large house, plenty of property and I don't have a job that takes me from home. We don't need the income, we'd be doing it for the right reasons and I think we have a lot to offer a kid like Carlo."

"I'll think about it, but it'll change our whole way of life. No more couch sex, or stairs sex, or porch sex, or kitchen table sex..."

"Yeah, I get that. It's not like the sex will stop though, just the random locations. This isn't something we *have* to do, just think about it." I didn't want to say it out loud but the idea of helping these kids and giving them a stable environment makes me happy. She nods and finishes her breakfast, but she's quiet the rest of the morning and goes to work without anything more to say about the subject.

QUINN

When Judson suggested a few days ago that we take on foster kids, it jumbled my mind. I've never thought about fostering before, but for a kid like Carlo, I think it would be worth the time and effort. His life would be so different if he were able to live in a place like ours with Judd and me as guardians. I don't think I'll have any issues getting approved but I'm not sure about Judson with his history of PTSD and drug and alcohol abuse. His being in treatment may work in his favor, especially if Dave will write him a recommendation.

Because I agreed to at least apply, Judson is going to see what he can do to start the process today. I wouldn't be jumping on this crazy train if it weren't for Carlo. Something about his situation and hope for the future brings out protective maternal instincts I thought didn't exist for me.

* * *

Two days later, the ringing of the phone pulls my concentration away from the paperwork I've been laboring over for the last hour.

"Officer Hannigan," a shrill female voice addresses me. "I'm Wilma Johnson, foster mother of Carlo Brown. We've got a problem and your partner said if I can't reach him to call you, no matter what."

"Yes, ma'am, that's correct. What's going on?" My heart rate picks up.

"Carlo is gone. He took off a couple of hours ago and I have no idea where he went. One of the other children that lives with us came to me a few minutes ago and said the drug dealer was coming for him and he was scared so he ran. Apparently he heard it at school. I don't know how but that's what this other child told me. Carlo made the boy promise not to tell anyone. I don't even know what drug dealer he's talking about. There's nothing in his file about drug issues. Do you know what he's talking about or where he might be?"

Shit. Dex is going to freak out. What the hell did we miss?

"Ms. Johnson, I'm not sure what's going on either but I'll locate my partner and we'll start looking. Please notify Ms. Winsted, the social worker. If you hear anything or he comes back, please call me."

"Okay, I will. I'm sorry, officer, I had no idea he might be a runner."

"I didn't know either." I hang up the phone and stride into the chief's office to let him know what's going on. He tells me to inform Dex and put out an alert. We pull the last four cases that involve his mother and review them, hoping to find something we missed. I text Dex to let him know he's needed as soon as he can get here. He took the afternoon off for personal reasons and I didn't ask why, but figure he'll want to help with this. Next, I text Judson and let him know I'll likely be late.

Three hours later, a search party has been combing the area near the foster home and his mother's apartment looking for Carlo, and the only thing I've discovered is Lateesha Brown is more tied to the local drug trade than we first suspected. Why Carlo didn't tell us, I have no idea. I leave the office and drive down to Lateesha's apartment. She's still in the ICU and it's unknown if she'll recover.

When I reach their apartment building, the old woman four

doors down is peering out the window as I pass. I give her a head nod and continue down the walkway. Thank goodness the locks on the doors here are crappy because it only takes me seconds to get inside. I cross the room and turn on the cheap ceramic lamp sitting on the rickety old end table by the hallway. Looking around the apartment, the only thing I see is broken furniture, a busted picture frame and small things scattered, presumably from the fight that put Lateesha in the ICU. I walk through both bedrooms and find more evidence of a struggle and piles of dirty clothes, but that's it. I'm not sure what I'm looking for, but I know I haven't found it. I turn off the lamp and lock the door behind me. This time, instead of walking past the old woman's apartment I stop to question her. I've noticed on previous visits she's always lurking behind the curtain like the neighborhood watchdog.

I knock on the door and it opens a crack. The old woman's eyes appear just below the chain that's pulled tight from the door to the wall inside.

"Ma'am, I'm looking for Carlo Brown. He ran away from his foster home and we're worried about him. Have you seen him here today?"

The old woman studies me for several seconds before she finally replies in an old, gravelly smoker's voice, "No, but he wouldn't come back here. He's too smart. It's possible he's in the park. I've heard some of the kids hide in the big sewage drain-pipe towards the back of the property when the weather is warmer like this. If you pick him up though, you'd better do right by him. He's a good boy, don't deserve none of what life gave him so far. Lateesha loves him, but has no business raising a child the way she lives and that daddy of his is a drug-dealing loser with no more than two pennies to rub together. If I find out you didn't do right by him, I'll go to the news. Seems all the news channels are real interested in stories of police neglect or brutality these days."

"Ma'am, I only want to help him. I'll look where you told me. Thank you."

"Don't thank me yet. I'm not certain you'll find him there, but I'm hopin' you will 'cause if not, it's likely D-Rock done found him already."

Shit. How does this old lady know about the drug dealer?

"How did you hear about D-Rock?"

"Everybody 'round here knows who the dope man is and when he's lookin' for someone, everybody gotta know. He's lookin' for Carlo so you best believe he tore through here already. That boy obviously knows somethin', but don't ask me what. I try to stay away from that stuff. Just pray Jesus will protect me from those bad people."

Shit, shit, shit. "Okay, thanks for your help."

She shuts the door and I can hear all three locks turn in place as I jog to the stairs. I need to get to the park before dark.

As I'm driving, Dex calls and I fill him in. "Sorry to ruin your afternoon off. I'm headed to the park to see if he's hiding in a drainage pipe. The old lady a few doors down told me I might find him there."

"Which park?" he asks, his voice tight. I rattle off the address and hang up.

Five minutes later, I'm surveying the park when Dex pulls in next to me. His long legs swing out of his vintage Dodge Charger before his body does. He's in jeans and a sweatshirt with a ball cap pulled low on his head.

"You see him?" he asks by way of greeting. I shake my head and return, "No, not yet. I was waiting for you before I trekked to the sewer pipe."

"Let's go then," he barks and takes off in a jog that borders on a run.

The cool air rushes across my face as we jog to the back of the property where this pipe is supposedly located. As we get close I can hear voices echoing inside. Dex steps in front of me and crouches down, pulling out a flashlight I didn't realize he had from the back of his jeans. As soon as the light hits the murky inside of the pipe, kids of all ages scatter like mice, running past us before we can talk to them. The second to last one out has a hoody pulled over his head but is the right height and build to be Carlo. I snatch him back to us by the neck of the hoody and he cries out. When he's close enough I yank the hood down to reveal our scrawny little friend, Carlo.

We got real freaking lucky he was in there. I was afraid we'd be looking all night for him. "What the hell were you thinking running away, boy?" Dex snarls at him.

Carlo's eyes narrow and he goes on the defensive. "I was thinkin' I don't want to die! D-Rock's after me. He's gonna get me. One of the kids at school told me he came looking for me. He's gonna whack me."

"What are you talking about?" I ask.

"D-Rock, he knows I saw him knock off that lady in the alley and he's looking for me to make sure I don't talk."

"Why didn't you tell us about this? We were with you just the other day."

"Growin' up 'round here I know to keep my mouth shut. I was hopin' he ain't see me or know who I was."

I look into his eyes, eyes that have seen more than any 10-year-old should ever see, and find absolute terror lurking in the chocolate depths. Placed in harm's way more often than not, he never feels safe, not having a clue what each day is going to hold. What Judson was saying to me smacks me upside the head like a frying pan. We have a lot to offer this kid and we have no reason not to do it. It would be selfish to ignore this opportunity and throw him back to the wolves. He could find safety out on our property, guarded by two people professionally trained to protect.

"Carlo, come out here with us. I need to talk to Dex a minute, okay? We're going to protect you. Just hang tight." He watches me, his expression thoughtful and still a little scared, until he finally nods. I usher him in front of me, away from the drain opening and away from the area. When we're far enough away I motion with my head to the left and Dex follows me, Carlo stays where I left him.

"I'm calling the social worker to see if Judson and I can get emergency guardianship."

Dex shakes his head. "That's a huge responsibility. You sure you want to take that on? This kid's not a stray dog. You can't take him in and then decide in a few days he's too much of a handful. That will make it worse for him. Besides, I'm not sure Judson will like it."

"Judson was already working on the paperwork and we were considering fostering. Now, with the danger Carlo's in, there's no better place for him to be than with a former Navy SEAL and a cop. Besides, then I don't have to worry what whacked-ass foster home he's going to end up in. If Lateesha lives through this, I'm not sure she'll be fit to take care of him anymore."

"I see your point. What can I do to help?"

"I don't know. Let's go find Ms. Winsted and figure this out."

Chapter Fourteen

QUINN

TWO DAYS, a thousand phone calls, a court appearance, a hundred conversations, and a ton of paperwork later and I'm driving up the lane to my house with Carlo in the car while Dex follows us. Carlo's quiet as he looks out the window.

Hoping not to startle him I ask, "You ever been this far out in the country?"

He shakes his head but doesn't reply.

"You okay, buddy?"

He glances at me and then back out the window. His eyebrows lower and pull together as he asks, "What if your man don't like me?"

"Why wouldn't he like you?"

"A lot of people don't like me. Maybe he won't like the way I look or somethin'." He shrugs.

"Judson's a good guy. You'll see. He was the one who suggested this in the first place. I think it'll be fine, but if it's not we'll talk about it and work it out. Our house isn't like any of the others you've been to, it's quiet. Just relax and we'll take it one day at a time."

He's silent again as we pull up in the driveway behind Judson's truck. I open the door and climb out. Carlo takes a moment before he opens his door and looks around. Dex strolls up to the passenger side and ruffles Carlo's hair. "Hey, kid. You ready?"

Carlo gives him a nervous nod and pushes the door closed. Dex leans down and whispers something to him and they smile at each other before they follow me to the back door, which is the one we use to enter and exit from.

"We're here!" I call out. The smell of spaghetti sauce and garlic fills the room and my stomach grumbles. I missed lunch trying to get out of work on time today for this. Judson strolls out of the kitchen and plants a chaste kiss on my lips before turning a wide smile to Dex and Carlo. He reaches his hand out to shake Dex's hand and then to Carlo to do the same. Carlo studies it for a second, unsure of what to do, I think.

Dex taps his shoulder and says, "Shake his hand. That's how men greet each other. Make sure it's firm and look him in the eye." Carlo glances back at Dex as he lifts his chin to him. Carlo swallows hard and shakes Judson's hand.

"Good to have you here. I made spaghetti, Quinn told me you like it. Let's put your stuff in your room and then we can eat and get to know each other."

I smile, realizing that Judson's obviously nervous too. He never talks this much around new people and only in the last four or five months has he started talking more to me.

Judd leads the way down the hall and shows Carlo to the room on the left that looks out to the barn and horse pen. I set Carlo's bag on the bed and make a mental note to take him shopping this weekend for some new clothes.

"This is where I'm sleepin'?" he asks, looking confused.

"Yeah, this is your room for as long as you're here. Is it okay?" Judson asks.

Carlo's eyes jump around the room, taking everything in. The queen-sized bed with the navy blue comforter, the matching desk and bedside table, the closet, the big window with grey curtains pulled back to allow the daylight in. The empty corkboard above the desk and the empty white walls.

"I know it's kind of bare in here but I thought you could decide what you wanted to hang on the walls instead of me putting something up you may not like. We'll figure it out as we go. For now, it's clean, it's safe, and you don't have to share with anyone. I just ask that you keep it picked up and keep your bed made when you're not in it."

Finally, Carlo smiles a real smile, first at Judson and then at Dex and me. "Okay. I can do that."

We all make our way to the kitchen and help Judson get the food on the table. Dinner starts out quiet, but it doesn't take long before conversation finds a rhythm between us. Carlo's particularly interested in Judson's military career so he shares the basics and handles the questions with patience. Carlo seems shocked by what he calls Judson's "fake leg" and even a little afraid of it, which makes Judd laugh hysterically.

The social worker, the principal, and Carlo's teacher decided it's a good idea to keep him out of school until this situation with D-Rock is under control. He's got a mound of work he'll be doing from home so that he doesn't fall behind. Judson and I agreed to help him with it and other than that he'll be getting acclimated to life on the ranch. I hope Judson's up for the challenge. I'm not sure this kid has ever seen any animals besides a cat or a dog. Maybe a bird or two, but not many inhabit the area he grew up in.

Later that evening, with Carlo tucked in bed, Judson and I are snuggled on the couch. His back to the corner, feet up on the coffee table, my body is nestled against him, legs stretched out down the couch. The fire is roaring next to us while the hockey game is turned down low on the television.

"You think he'll be okay here?" I ask Judson.

"Yeah, Daisy, I do. He's never been anywhere like this place. Just needs some time. I've got plenty to give him. You're off for a four-day stretch after the weekend. It'll be fine."

"You seem certain."

"We're good people. We take care of ourselves and those we care about. We're both strong, making it through tough things in life. We're both educated and come from good homes. He's never had any of that. From what you say about his mom she's a nice person, but not much going for her past that, and his dad isn't even worth mentioning. It'll be fine, just an adjustment."

"Okay. Have I told you today how much I love you?" I question softly.

"Nope, but I'm ready to listen," he grins cheekily.

I smack his chest playfully and say, "I love you a lot."

He kisses my hair and rubs my arm. "I love you too, Daisy." Without another word he turns off the TV and carries me to our room. After shutting our door, he places me on the bed, strips off my clothes and spends the next hour quietly showing me how much he loves me.

JUDSON

This morning as I'm making Quinn breakfast, a sleepy Carlo wanders out in a T-shirt and ragged pajama pants that are probably a size too small. "Hey, buddy. You hungry?"

He nods his head but doesn't say anything, obviously not a morning person.

"Okay, I'm making bacon and scrambled eggs. Do you eat those?" Another affirmative nod. Not a big talker in the morning. I smile to myself and finish cooking.

After breakfast, Quinn leaves and I sit down at the table with Carlo to tell him the schedule. Everything I've read says that kids need a schedule so they know what to expect. Supposedly, it helps to reduce anxiety in new situations. When I called my mom to tell her what we were doing and ask her to come by this weekend to meet him, she said the same thing so I made a written schedule he could follow.

I slide the schedule across the table and explain, "Most of the time during the week, this is what our schedule will look like until you go back to school. On occasion we may have to change plans, but on a normal basis this is it. Why don't you look at it and let me know if you have any questions."

He looks it over and comments, "I've never been around horses before. Only seen 'em on TV. I don't know what to do with them."

"That's okay. I'm going to teach you. It'll take you a little time to get used to them, but they're pretty cool. Just follow directions and don't stand behind them. I don't want you to get kicked on accident." His eyes widen but he doesn't respond so I tell him, "When I give you directions I want to know you've heard them, so please say, 'yes, sir' or 'no, sir.' Okay?"

He stares at me for a full minute before he says, "Yes, sir." Okay, so his mom hasn't taught him basic manners. This will be interesting.

We spend the morning feeding and exercising the horses and the time after lunch doing schoolwork and talking. He's a smart kid, but a little rough around the edges. Nothing a little time, care and attention won't fix. When preparation begins for dinner I allow him to help, giving him instructions on how to do each thing. When Quinn walks through the door, Carlo proudly announces that he's helped with the horses and dinner. The smile he grants her after excitedly sharing details about his day fills me with pride. Even more so than the last several months of repairs on the barn.

When dinner's over we wash the dishes and watch television for an hour before it's time for Carlo to go to bed. While Quinn is showering, I watch the end of the hockey game in our room. When she strolls out of the bathroom in a light pink tank top and short, pink, plaid pajama shorts, I know we won't be sleeping anytime soon. Her dark hair is pulled back in a ponytail with little wisps of hair escaping around her face. Her blue eyes shine bright with happiness. She finishes rubbing the lotion into her hands and crawls across the bed toward me like a cat on the prowl. Even after all the women I've been with she's still the sexiest of them all, without even trying. Maybe that's part of it.

I reach up and trace my fingers down her cheek to her jaw. "Beautiful. No one I've ever been with is more beautiful than you are," I confess. "How did I get so lucky?"

She turns into my hand and kisses my palm, holding her lips there for several long seconds. She shifts her weight and moves between my legs, planting a kiss on my chest, then moves down and places one over my nipple, surprising me with a swipe of her tongue before she pulls away and switches to the other one. This time she takes it between her teeth and tugs a little. A groan slips out of my mouth and my head falls back to clunk on the headboard.

"Quinn..."

Her finger covers my lips. "Shhh."

My tongue swipes out and licks her finger. A wicked grin spreads across her luscious lips and I know immediately what she wants. Hooking her fingers in my pajama pants, she pulls them down and drops them to the floor. Commando underneath, my straining cock pops out and snaps to my stomach with a smack. Her cool palm cups my sac as she massages me with gentle hands.

"Feels so good, Daisy," I murmur. Her mouth drops close enough for me to feel her breath but not close enough to touch. I twitch in response. Her tongue snakes out and slithers from root to tip and swirls the head. I force myself to hold still as I watch. She repeats the process in reverse and squeezes my balls at the same time. My eyes roll back in my head as my breath quickens. She releases them and slips that hand up my bare abs in a whisper-light touch, the other grips my cock and the head disappears between her lips into the warm, wet depths of her mouth. She works me slow with a twist of her wrist and a twirl of her tongue every time and my legs tense. Her eyes are closed as she puts all of her effort into this. It's both heaven and hell. I can feel a buzzing pressure at the base of my spine spreading to my balls, but I'm not ready to come so I wrap her ponytail around my fist and pull her away. With a loud pop she releases me and her eyes focus on mine.

"You didn't like what I was doing?" she asks, her voice sexy in a breathy kind of way.

I groan. "I love it, but I'm not ready to come and that's where you're taking me."

She flashes her wicked grin at me before her tongue slides out again and swipes at the head of my dick. Good God, that feels so awesome.

"I don't want to stop. Don't I get a say?" she queries. "I want more." Her tongue laps at me again, as her eyes implore me to give in.

My grip on her hair loosens because I can't remember why I was holding out. It makes no sense. "Go ahead, Daisy. If it makes you happy, by all means, have at it."

She doesn't respond, she just ducks her head and goes back to work, her eyes never leaving mine this time. As my orgasm builds, stronger this time, my toes curl, one hand in her ponytail and the other on her neck, pressing her further down on me. Her eyes water a little at the pressure so I release her. She backs off, takes a breath and slides back down, stretching her lips and relaxing her throat. The visual sends me over the edge and I warn, "I'm coming, Daisy."

She doesn't pull away. She swallows as I lose it, coating her throat. When my cock stops pulsing she lets it slip between her lips and smiles at me.

"You're gonna kill me, woman," I tell her, exhausted now.

"I don't want you to die, but death by orgasm seems like the way to go, don't you think?" She laughs hysterically as she crawls up to the pillow and lays her head down. I slip my arm behind her and pull her close to me, thinking this may have been the best day of my life so far.

* * *

A week passes and life continues on in a good way. Carlo is settled into a routine around the house and seems to be calmer than when he arrived. When Quinn had her days off from work, we left the ranch to hike at a nearby park and had dinner at a little hole-in-the-wall restaurant on the outskirts of town. Dex joining us for the outing made Carlo happier than I'd seen him yet.

The best part of the last week came though when we got Carlo on a horse for his first ride. The kid was scared out of his mind. The size of the horses seems to intimidate him so he's given them a wide berth but we made him do this. I figured if he was mucking stalls, feeding and helping to brush them down, he should at least get a chance to experience the good part about having them. It took a little while of Quinn working with him for him to relax but he finally did and we actually heard him laugh for the first time during that initial ride. Now, every day, I get him on one. He's still not experienced enough to use the more difficult parts of the trail so we're sticking close to the house. In a few weeks that won't be an issue anymore and we'll be able to tour the whole property.

Carlo is working on his math homework when my cell phone rings, the caller ID indicates it's Quinn.

"Hey, Daisy."

"Hey, honey. I need you to step out of the room if you're with Carlo."

I tell Carlo, "I'll be back in a few minutes, buddy. You're doing well. Just make sure you show all the steps and you'll do fine. I'll check it when I come back." He nods his understanding and I walk back to our bedroom.

"What's up?"

"I just got a report that D-Rock is dead at a motel in Castle Rock. I'll be late getting home so go ahead and eat without me. We're waiting for visual confirmation before I leave for the night. I have no idea how long it'll take. Did Ms. Winsted call you today?"

"She did. There's been no change with Lateesha."

"Okay. I'll see you in a little while."

We hang up and I return to the kitchen table to check on Carlo. He's still quietly working.

*　*　*

Two hours later, we're finishing dinner when a loud boom followed by a whoosh sound, rocks the house from the outside in the direction of the barn. I dart to the window and see flames shooting 50 feet in the air above the ramshackle shed next to the barn. There's nothing in the shed that would cause an explosion like the one we just heard. In fact, the shed is empty because that was my next project and Carlo helped me with that yesterday. My gut sours. My heart rate picks up and I turn to Carlo, standing about two feet behind me, his eyes are as round as saucers, and his gaze is locked on the flame-engulfed shed. That fire didn't set itself and I don't want him to encounter whoever did it. I also need to make sure those flames don't jump to the barn with the horses.

"Lock the door behind me and call 911. Tell them there's a fire on the property and we aren't sure what caused it. Tell them I'm outside trying to put out the blaze and I have my gun on me just in case. Do you understand?" He nods quickly, terror obvious in his eyes.

"Go!" I bark. Then I run to my room and grab my 9mm from the safe under the bed, pop in the clip and shove it in the back of my jeans as I turn and sprint outside. I hear the click as the door locks behind me and I glance back to see Carlo's wide eyes following me through the window panes in the door, phone to his ear, mouth moving. I run to the water hose and turn it on full blast, scanning the property around me as I do. I see nothing, but it's dark and there are a lot of hiding spots on this ranch. A motion sensor floodlight pops on over in the side yard and I spin to see a shadow shift back toward the house. I back out of the light into the shadows and lower the hose to the ground, hoping it will wet the grass enough so the dry grass between the shed and barn doesn't catch on fire and spread.

What the hell am I gonna do? I have to get across the yard and back into the house with Carlo. A crash that sounds like breaking glass comes from the front of the house and my head swings around to see that Carlo is no longer in the window watching me. I stop debating on what to do and pull my piece as I sprint for the house.

What the fuck is going on? Of course the door is locked on the backside because I asked him to do that for me. *Shit.* I look through the windows and see nothing. While running for the side yard I smack into a large form along the edge of the house. We both go down in a heap and my gun flies out of my hand.

I throw a punch and dodge one at the same time. By the feel of him, we're about the same size. I barely clip the guy and he misses me all together. I roll him to his back and pound on his face with concentrated force. His swings are wild in return but two of those connect, knocking me a little senseless for a few seconds, just long enough for him to flip me and rain punches in my midsection and one more to my face. I can't get the traction I need to buck him off because of the leg. I reach up and grab his neck with both hands and smash my forehead to his, knocking him stupid long enough to throw him off. He hits the ground with a thud and a groan, gripping his bloody forehead, and I roll quickly and army-crawl along the ground the two feet to where he rolled. He's still dazed and moaning in pain so I lock my hands around his neck and squeeze for all it's worth.

I can hear the click of a switchblade pop open as he struggles against me and I shift my attention toward the sound just in time to see the silver glint of the sharp blade in the light and feel the burn as it slices my arm. I squeeze tighter hoping he'll pass out before he gets to me again. Attempting to take away his range of motion with the blade, I lean toward the side, putting pressure on his bicep, and it works for a few seconds. His body jerks toward the other side throwing me off balance enough for his arm to swing again. This time the blade sticks in my forearm and I let go of his neck to plow a punch in his face with my uninjured arm.

He finally loses consciousness so I yank out the blade and flip it closed. I roll him to his stomach, tug off my belt and use it to secure his arms behind his back. He's breathing, but out cold. My arm's on fire where the blade first sliced me but I don't have time to worry about it. Once he's secure, I run for the house, certain he's not the only one here. *Who the fuck are these people?*

When I reach the front porch I see glass scattered all over like someone knocked it in and used the small opening to unlock the door. I tiptoe inside, scanning as I proceed, moving from room to room. There's no one in this part of the house so I creep into the library and grab the other gun safe I have hidden, since my gun is in the grass somewhere, and remove my Glock. I load it and move back to the hall as quietly as I can. One bum leg is not making a stealth approach easy.

Carlo's terrified shriek rings through the house and a fear I've never felt in my life shoots through my body, activating my adrenaline again. I give up on quiet and sprint to his room, throwing my shoulder into his door as I go. The door pops right open and I stumble in.

The biggest black guy I've ever seen in my life is standing over a sobbing Carlo with a gun pointed at his head, execution style. Both sets of eyes jump to mine and before anyone can make a peep I aim and fire right between the eyes of the guy with the gun. Carlo screams, dropping to the floor face-first as the man jerks and drops on top of him. Hysterical screaming fills the air and I scramble to roll the guy off of Carlo. The big guy is gone, dead as a doornail. I've never been happier in my life to have perfect marksmanship. I tug Carlo to me and wrap my arms around him. He's still screaming.

"Shhh. Shhh. Carlo. Stop. I need you to tell me if there are any more." He's still screaming, but not as loud or as consistently. "Carlo," I squeeze tight and command, "tell me, are there any more of these guys?" His head shakes back and forth quickly and the screaming turns to a keening sound I hope I never have to hear again in my life.

"Okay, buddy. It's okay. It's over. I need you to calm down. There's another guy in the yard I have tied up, but I need to check on him, okay? Come with me. Close your eyes and climb up in my arms. I'll carry you. It's gonna be okay." I stand, my legs shaking as the adrenaline exits my system as fast as it came. Carlo jumps right up in my arms and wraps his little kid legs around my waist. I grip his thighs and limp my way out to the living room. The fire is almost out and doesn't seem to have spread to the barn. Thank God.

I carry him outside and see the man's feet kicking and pushing like he's trying to get up or get to something so I set Carlo down and say, "Get against the house by the door and crouch down. I've got to take care of that guy."

"Yessss, yessss, sir." His whole body is shaking. His little legs buckle and he stumbles to the side of the house where I told him to go. I hustle down the stairs to the man on his belly. He's now rolled to a weird angle. I'm almost to him when he lifts his hands the little bit the belt will allow and I realize what he was crawling to, a little too late. My 9mm catches the light and he fires two in a row. I dive left just as a searing pain burns through my right shoulder and then in my gut.

Carlo is screaming again and the sound draws the attention of the man with the gun wiggling to get to his feet. *Fuck!* I force myself up and tackle him, holding my body over his. I can feel both hands and know the gun isn't in them, but I have no idea where it is. About that time, I can hear the sirens quickly approaching as the emergency crews speed up the driveway. The man under me panics and swings his head back, connecting with mine, and everything goes black.

Chapter Fifteen

QUINN

A COUPLE of hours after I speak to Judson, a picture of the dead guy pops up on my phone and I'm expecting to see D-Rock. It's not D-Rock. It's just some poor schmuck with a bullet between the eyes, who happened to drive the same type of car as D-Rock and be approximately the same size and race. We're back to square one of trying to find this guy. He went to ground around the time Carlo moved in with us and no one has seen him who's willing to admit it.

I turn to Dex, "It's not D-Rock. I don't know who this joker is, but it's not him. Let's go home for the night. I'm done." He nods and stands, grabbing his coat from the back of his chair. As I'm holding up my phone to show Dex the picture, it rings. I answer and it's Gary from dispatch.

"We've just dispatched to your address. A kid called in a fire on the property and said your man was outside with a gun. I don't know what's going on but you'd better get there."

Terror floods my system. I don't say a word as I hit end on the call and sprint through the office with Dex on my heels yelling at me to stop.

"I can't. Carlo called in a fire on the property and Judson's outside with a gun. I don't know what the hell is going on but I'm leaving."

I jump in the squad car since it's closest and fire it up. Dex hurls himself inside as I'm peeling out of the space. We haul ass all the way to my house, coming in right behind the fire truck and police car they dispatched. An ambulance pulls in behind me as we hit the last part of gravel driveway leading to the house going 60 miles per hour. Halfway up there's an older model, shiny emerald green, pimped-out Chevy Impala pulled off to the side, lights out.

"Who the hell is that?" I blurt.

Dex doesn't bother responding.

A second later we barrel into the driveway. I throw the car into park and jump out, running for the back door, and that's when I hear the screaming from the other side of the back porch. Smoke is heavy in the air and the shed is burnt almost all the way to the ground. I pull my gun and keep running. I assume the owner of the heavy footsteps behind me is Dex. My heart stops when I round the porch and find Carlo holding the limp hand of a bloody Judson, looking like a scene from a war movie. I drop to my knees by Judson's head.

"Oh God! Oh God! Oh God! Don't die. Don't die." I push my fingers to his neck looking for a pulse and feel the warm blood covering his skin. Carlo's cries grow louder across from me.

"Oh God. Oh God!" I can't find the right spot or he's dead, I don't know which and I'm hysterical. Dex yanks Carlo back into his arms and turns away, attempting to calm him. The paramedics push me out of the way and start to work on Judson. The cop who pulled in before us wraps his arms around me and pulls me away saying, "Let them work. It's going to be okay. Let them work."

It takes a second for me to stop struggling and scan the area. Three feet away is another man down with his arms at a weird angle behind his back. One of the paramedics is working on him.

He has a gunshot wound to the leg, a bloody face from a huge gash in his forehead, but is still conscious and cussing.

"Did you shoot him, you piece of shit?" I scream at the bastard on the ground. "I'll kill you with my bare hands," I continue, and do my best to pull away from the officer holding me. I'm held tighter. "Let me go!" I screech.

"Hannigan, calm down. Not gonna happen. Not letting you go. Calm down."

About that time the paramedic yells, "We've got a pulse, let's move." They grab the board Judson's now strapped on and lift him into the ambulance, flip the lights and sirens back on, circle the driveway and pull off faster than they were driving to get here.

"What about me?" the asshole on the ground shouts.

"Unfortunately, you'll live. I've got another one coming for you soon," the paramedic replies.

It suddenly occurs to me that Carlo was kneeling next to Judson.

"Carlo," I yell. "Carlo, are you okay? Let me go. I need to get to him!" I wrench free and run to where Dex is holding Carlo in his lap on the steps of my back porch. Another cop is standing close by, but isn't saying anything. I drop to my knees and wrap my arms around them both.

"Are you okay? Did he hurt you?"

"I'm sorry I couldn't save him. I'm sorry!" he wails.

Perplexed, I pull away and look up at him. "Save who? What are you talking about?"

Dex speaks up. "He thinks he should have saved Judson."

"Oh God, Carlo, no. It's his job to protect you, not you to protect him. You did well. You got help here. It's going to be okay. We'll go to the hospital. It'll be okay."

"I didn't listen. I didn't listen."

"What do you mean?"

"He told me to stay by the house, but when the man shot him

I had to help. I found the gun on the ground and I shot that dude, but I couldn't save Judson."

"Oh my gosh. You shot the man over there with his hands behind his back?"

"Yes," he cries harder.

"It's okay. It's okay." I do my best to soothe him. "Are you hurt? Who's that guy? Do you know him?"

He shakes his head. "No, but D-Rock is in the house. He's dead. Judson killed him." The horror Judson and Carlo experienced washes over me and I wrap my arms tighter around Carlo and Dex. My limbs begin to shake and it's not long before I can't hold myself up.

Dex's deep voice grounds me. "Quinn, get it together. We need to go to the hospital. I'll drive."

He's right. I pull away as I continue to shake, nodding. I need to be there for Judson.

"Yo! Rogers! Taking these two to the hospital. You got questions, you meet us there," Dex yells over to the officer cuffing the guy on the ground as the paramedic tries to stop the bleeding from the gunshot wound Carlo apparently gave him.

"Oh, and check in the house. The boy says Demarius Jenkins, aka D-Rock, is dead in there somewhere. Said Mr. Rivers killed him."

Officer Rogers's eyes widen as he nods and strides past us into the house. Everyone in law enforcement in this town knows who D-Rock is, so I'm sure he's more than surprised to hear this news.

Dex drives as I ride in the backseat with my arm around Carlo. His tears have stopped but his sniffles haven't.

"Carlo, when the officers come to the hospital you'll have to tell us the story of what happened, okay?"

He nods.

"You sure it was D-Rock in that room?"

He nods again but doesn't say a word. I squeeze him to me and we continue the ride in silence.

When we arrive in the emergency room waiting area, the receptionist takes one look at us and gestures for us to step in to the triage area. It's oddly empty here tonight and I'm so thankful for that.

"Is he hurt?" the receptionist asks me, her eyes locked on the blood that seems to be covering Carlo from head to toe. He doesn't answer. I'm a little worried he's going into shock. He's seen so much in his life and I'm afraid this may be what breaks him.

"I don't know. I don't think so. Can we have him examined to be sure? I'm not sure he could even tell us right now."

"Yes, let me get a nurse and we'll handle this. Just relax in that chair for now."

After I'm seated in the plastic chair, I look around the tiny room noticing the blood pressure cuff, the small cart with bandages and gauze, the little cart with the digital thermometer, the metal desk next to me and the stool rolled up under it. The walls are clinical white, the room sterile. I pull Carlo to my lap and hold him close to me and hope nothing from my uniform scratches him. "Are you hurt, buddy?" He shakes his head but doesn't speak. "Where is all this blood coming from?" I ask.

"D-Rock," is the only word he says. I have no idea what that means but I don't push him. The receptionist returns with a young nurse in green scrubs and she says, "Hi, I'm Melanie. We're going to skip triage and take you to an open bed in the back. No need to poke and prod him more than once if we don't have to."

I'm grateful for the calming presence of the sweet young nurse.

After Carlo's been examined and it's been determined that the blood is not his, we're led into a small private conference room I imagine they use for speaking to families when they have to deliver bad news. Dex's huge body dwarfs the metal folding chair he's seated on. Carlo is between us with his head resting on his crossed arms on the table. The social worker and a detective are on their way to question us. I'm so afraid of what will come out of Carlo's mouth. I'm afraid of what he witnessed. Judson's in surgery now. They had a problem stopping the bleeding from the wound to his abdomen. I'm trying not to think about that as we wait. If I let too much come to mind, I'll lose it and I can't afford that with Carlo to take care of. At least he's still alive, I remind myself. Judson's lived through worse and he's strong and healthy now. It's going to be okay.

The frumpy social worker pushes through the door first and takes in the scene with assessing eyes. I'm sure she's wondering why Carlo's in a hospital gown and I dread telling her it's because his clothes were too bloody to wear.

"What happened?" she blurts.

I shake my head. "He's not answering any questions until we're all together. I don't want him repeating it again and again. The detective should be here any minute. I can tell you that he was at home with Judson alone when everything happened. I was working late. In fact, I think me working late was a diversion of some sort."

"Well, I have to file a report and get him assigned to another home for tonight if he's free to leave when we're through."

My hackles rise like a pissed off pooch. "He's not going to another home. We'll stay in a hotel until the house is cleaned up, but he's not going anywhere. I'm sure you mean well, but I won't let anything happen to him and I'm not sure anyone else can say the same."

"Well, we are in a hospital having this conversation, officer, so I'm not thinking you can honestly say you'll keep him safe."

"Ms. Winsted, I can promise you this, if he was anywhere else when all of this happened you'd be burying him instead of interviewing him. I have no doubt Judson did everything in his power to keep Carlo safe."

She crosses her arms over her chest and sits back, realizing

I'm not in the mood to be messed with. She'll have to peel Carlo from my cold dead hands. He's not going anywhere.

Within 15 minutes the detective arrives and we all listen to Carlo tell what happened. I can't help the tears when he explains how Judson saved him and how he got pinned under D-Rock's dead body. The worst though is when he picked up the gun and saved Judson. By the time he's finished, both my despair for Judson and my pride in Carlo's quick thinking and selflessness has grown. Now, I just need for Judson to be okay and I need to call his mom and brother.

* * *

Hours later, Judson's brother, mother, Ms. Polly, Dex, Carlo, our chief, and a few guys from the department are all in the waiting room with us. Ms. Polly stopped and bought Carlo some clothes so he didn't have to wear the gown, and he's resting with his head against Dex's shoulder, eyes closed. I would say he's sleeping but every time the door from the back swings open, his eyes flip open and he watches for the doctor.

In my boredom, I've noted every dust bunny in the corners, each handprint on the wall near the bathroom and the number of times Judson's brother has paced in front of me. Stir crazy doesn't even begin to touch what I'm feeling right now.

About the time I'm contemplating taking a walk outside, a tall, thin gentleman with a long face wearing scrubs and a blue hair cover pushes through the double doors and looks around the room before he announces, "Family for Rivers." We all push forward and the doctor looks a little alarmed by our reaction.

Looking at Mrs. Rivers he asks, "Are you Mr. Rivers's mother?" She nods. Tears are pooling in her eyes but it looks like by the firm set of her jaw, she's fighting them.

"Mr. Rivers made it through. He lost a lot of blood and it was touch and go for a bit, but he's a fighter. How long ago did he lose his leg?" Mrs. Rivers looks like if she opens her mouth to answer, she's going to lose it, so I answer, "About two years ago. Combat. IED. He was a Navy SEAL."

"I saw the tattoo so I guessed that was the case. Are you his wife?"

"No, sir. I'm his domestic partner." This is the first time I've ever used that term and felt like an idiot. *Why did I refuse to get married again?*

"Do you have paperwork as his power of attorney?"

Shaking my head, I respond, "No, sir. We haven't made it that far."

"I hate to tell you this but with the HIPAA laws I won't be able to share any of the information with you unless he wakes up and authorizes it." Damn it. Another reason I should have made this official. *Why am I so damn stubborn?*

"Mrs. Rivers, you can share whatever you want with whomever you want but as his next of kin you will be who our staff communicates with and you'll have to make any necessary decisions should they arise. I'm sorry to put this all on you. You're more than welcome to confer with your family, but I'm only allowed to communicate with you until he tells me otherwise."

"I understand. When can we see him?" she asks.

"Once they get him settled in the ICU I will let a couple of you go in to see him. I'm sorry but the boy won't be able to go in. Hospital policy."

I send Carlo home with Dex and they follow Ms. Polly to make sure she gets home okay. The chief and the guys we work with leave us for the night and the only ones of us that remain are his brother, his mom and me.

It was the second longest night of my life. The first being in Germany when he cried out in pain all night long. Thank God I know he's tough or I'd be a basket case by now. When we go in to see him there are wires and tubes everywhere. The covers are pulled all the way up to his neck so I can't see any signs of the mess his body is below.

* * *

Late the next afternoon, Judson finally wakes up and asks for me. Dex has Carlo with him and I've refused to leave the hospital since I arrived, so now almost 24 hours later, I look like shit. I follow the nurse into the room and step right up next to the bed. His eyes are droopy like he's sleepy and a small smile tips his lips.

"Judson," I whisper before I burst into tears.

He pulls his hand out from under the covers and reaches for me. "Don't cry, Daisy. I'm okay. Is Carlo okay?"

I nod quickly and say, "Yeah, he's staying with Dex until we're ready to take him back. You saved him. He only had a few bruises and some sore muscles from where D-Rock landed on him."

"Good, but I was more worried about if he is okay in the head. He killed that guy. It's the last thing I remember."

"He didn't kill him. Just wounded him. Carlo's shaken up but he's okay. He'll be glad you're awake. How do you feel?"

"Like shit."

"I'll call your mom in a minute. I sent her and your brother home a few hours ago to get cleaned up and get some rest. They're worried something would happen and no one would tell me since we aren't married."

His brow furrows but he says nothing. He's probably exhausted.

"I love you, Judson. I was so scared."

"I know, Daisy, me, too."

His grip on my hand loosens as he drifts back off to sleep. I stay with him a little bit longer and then call everyone to let them know he's awake.

EPILOGUE

QUINCY

It's been three months since the shooting and things are changing in our house. Judson is finally back to working in the stable and on the property. With rehab, he's getting stronger every day. Gone is the quiet somber man I've always known, replaced by the sexy, smiling, share-happy man seated at the kitchen table talking animatedly with Carlo. Sure, he's still a good listener, able to shut his mouth long enough to absorb what another person is saying, but now his feelings come out often. He never misses a moment to tell me he loves me or appreciates me and has become vocal with Carlo too on those issues. What those two went through together that day bonded them for life. Carlo is back in counseling for that incident and everything else he's faced in his young life.

His mother woke up from her coma with her mental capacity severely diminished. She'll never be able to take care of herself, much less her son again, and after a long discussion with Carlo, the counselor, and the social worker, we petitioned the state to adopt him permanently. We're waiting for the paperwork to go through but the lawyer says he doesn't see an issue. We take Carlo to see Lateesha once a week at a nursing home in the city. It's always difficult but we don't want to cut her out of his life. He still needs to see her.

Right now I'm sitting on some major news like a mother goose on an egg and it's making me antsy. We're all in the kitchen preparing for breakfast.

"Daisy, you listening?" Judson asks from the table.

"Um...sorry I was off in la-la land."

His forehead wrinkles. "You okay?"

"Yes, yes, I'm fine. What were you saying?"

He rolls his eyes like a petulant teenager and says, "With Carlo's birthday coming up I think we should have a big party here at the house. Invite the family and he can invite his friends from school. The boys could stick around afterwards and we could do a campout by the pond. I'm sure we could get Dex to join us and maybe even Joel and his son."

I glance over to Carlo, trying to judge his thoughts on this and am happy to find him sitting enthusiastically on the edge of his chair, hands clasped together pleading for a yes.

"Carlo, what do you think?" I prompt, already knowing what he's thinking.

"Yes, yes, yes! Please, Quinn? I've never had a campout or a party before."

My heart falls a little at his declaration. A kid his age shouldn't just now be getting his first birthday party.

I nod my head. "I think we can handle that. When are you thinking of doing this? I work the weekend before your birthday and am off the weekend after. If you want Dex there, you have to do it when we're off. Think you can wait?"

Carlo springs from his chair like a jack-in-the-box and rushes to me, throwing his arms around my waist. "I can wait till after. It's really okay?"

Smoothing my hand over his head, I respond, "If it will make you happy, I'm in!"

He releases me and jumps across the kitchen in excited kid fashion, pumping his fist.

I glance over at Judd and he winks at me.

* * *

Later that day Judson and I are out on the property riding Comet and Jasper. Judson stops us at the highest point we can get to by horse and dismounts. He rubs Comet affectionately while I join him. We stand there overlooking our land. Everything is green right now except the large patches of white daisies that started to bloom a few weeks ago. There are some other colorful wildflowers blooming but the daisies dominate the open spaces. Judson was right when he told me all those years ago how beautiful they were.

Glancing at him as he observes the countryside, I turn my focus back to the daisies. "How do you think you'll like fatherhood?" His eyes never move but a small smile plays on his lips as he answers. "I think it will be just fine. Did I tell you that he asked to hyphenate his last name?"

"He did?" I ask, surprised.

"Yeah, he wants to be a Rivers but was afraid to abandon his mom so he asked if he could be Rivers-Brown since Brown-Rivers sounded like diarrhea. His words, not mine." I bust up laughing at the comment. I guess that's what you get from an almost 11-year-old boy.

"Well, what do you think he'll say about a brother or sister?" I'm doing everything I can to fight the smile trying to take over my face.

"I have to be honest, Daisy, I don't think I can take on another foster kid or even adopt right now. Maybe in a few months. Why? Is there a kid you're attached to that we need to take in?"

Tears well in my eyes. I get to tell him something I never thought I'd be able to say in my life and the hormones have me extra emotional on top of that.

My lips quiver as I reply, "No, there is no other kid to foster." I reach out and grip his hand. His left eyebrow rises as he focuses on me. The tears spill over my lids and run down my cheeks.

"Judd, I'm pregnant."

A myriad of emotions zip across his features until he finally stops at the one I was hoping for...a smile. Bright and beautiful and happy.

"You? But I thought..." he trails off.

"Yes, me. I went to the doctor this week. I haven't been feeling well but didn't want to alarm you so I went on my lunch break. The urine test came back positive in his office so he did blood work and an exam, it's confirmed. Judson, we're going to have a baby. I'm 11 weeks along. I'm considered a high-risk pregnancy though so I have to be careful and will be pulled for desk duty sooner rather than later."

He lets out a whoop you'd expect in an old cowboy movie, startling the horses, and pulls me tight to him. I continue to cry because I'm a big emotional baby these days as he kisses my head and holds me tight.

"Eleven weeks? That's almost three months. How did you not know before?"

"I thought I couldn't get pregnant so I was blaming the crappy feeling on stress. I haven't thrown up but I have felt nauseous and tired."

"Why didn't you tell me sooner?" I can hear the slight irritation in his voice.

"I wanted to make sure it was real and I wanted to do it while we were alone. I figure we'll need to talk to the counselor about how to discuss this with Carlo. I'm not sure how he'll take it."

"Best day of my life," he murmurs against my hair.

JUDSON

She's going to have my baby. I never thought I'd see the day. I was excited to adopt Carlo and was content with that, but her news changes everything for me. The best part is about to happen though because I brought her up here on this overlook, before I knew about the baby, for the sole purpose of asking her to marry me. She's been crying into my shirt for the last five minutes so I grip her arms and push her back a little so I can look at her tear-stained face.

"Daisy, I brought you up here for my own selfish reasons. You told me several times when we first got together that you wouldn't marry me because we couldn't have a family. Carlo changed that when we decided to adopt him."

It takes me a second but I finally get on one knee and dig the little black box out of my pocket. I tug her hand forward gently and kiss her fingers.

"Daisy, we're about to be a family of four. Your former logic no longer holds, so you know the answer I'm expecting, right?" Her tears are back, running in heavy streams down her face. Her nose is red and her lip is quivering. She nods a little.

"I love you more than I've ever loved anything. I've wanted you in one shape or form since the moment I saw you, but for today and the rest of our lives, I want you to be my wife. I'll do my best to give you everything you've ever wanted."

Her head begins to nod so hard she looks like a dashboard bobblehead on a bumpy road.

"Yes!" her voice comes out strained but excited.

I open the box and pull out the ring that was my mother's. It's only a one-karat princess cut with baguettes on each side but it's still beautiful and perfect for her little hand.

Her eyes widen. "Your mother's ring?"

"If you want your own we can go looking on your next day off. This one just meant something to me so I asked my mom for it."

"God! I love it. No, I don't need another ring." Her response is one of the things I love about her. There's no muss, no fuss, what you see is what you get. Beautiful, classy but casual, easy to please, straightforward, hard-working and sexy. You can't find women like that anywhere anymore. I'm so damn lucky.

CARLO: SEVEN YEARS LATER

I step up to the podium and scan through the crowd, finding my whole family, plus Ms. Polly in her wheelchair and Dex and his family. I deliberately make eye contact with Judson first, then Quinn, next is Dex and finally with my little sister, Lila. She's squirming in her seat like little kids do when they're bored, until I wink at her. Then she straightens her back, sits up tall and flashes me a smile most jack-o'-lanterns would be proud of. I chuckle softly into the microphone before I start my speech.

"Hello, my name is Carlo Rivers-Brown. I was told being the class valedictorian required me to give a speech. As most of you know, I have no problem talking, to or in front of people, but I knew this speech would be hard. If you haven't heard my story, let me give you a quick overview to bring you up to speed. I was born to a poor single mother and an abusive drug-dealing father. Until I was 10 years old, I was in and out of foster care as my mother was in and out of jail and the hospital. To make a long story short, Officer Hannigan, now Rivers, and Officer Dexter responded to several calls at my apartment and took a special interest in me.

"Before it was all said and done, I was adopted by Judson and Quincy Rivers officially, and unofficially by Officer Dexter. They became my family. I got lucky when my little sister, Lila, was born and I learned what it was like to love someone more than myself for no other reason than just because she existed. If it weren't for those people and their families taking me in, loving me and setting a good example of what honorable people are like, I wouldn't be standing here today.

"They saved me, both in the figurative and literal sense of the word. Today, I want to dedicate this accomplishment to Judson, Quincy, Dex, and Lila. You changed my life the day you found me on that closet floor and again when you found me in the sewage drain. I'll do everything I can to make you proud and to pay forward everything you've given me. I promise to find the purpose in my life and work hard for it." I swallow hard, trying not to cry. My buddies would never let me live that shit down.

I focus back on the crowd as a whole and away from Quincy's face. I can't stand to see her cry and of course she is. She acts tough but she's a serious softie. I finish my speech with an attempt to motivate my fellow classmates about their future, and return to my seat. When the graduation ceremony is over and I'm through taking pictures with my family, an older white-haired man in a Navy dress uniform, layered heavily with medals, approaches us. Judson straightens next to me and smiles at him. The man stops in front of us and shakes Judson's outstretched hand.

Judd speaks first, "Sir, I'd like you to meet my son, Carlo." He looks to me and back to the man with obvious pride in his eyes. I'll never get tired of that.

"Carlo, this is Commander Hayden." My gut clenches a bit. I owe this man big time. How do I convey that without coming across like an idiot?

I thrust my hand in front of me and he grasps it firmly and shakes. "It's a pleasure," he says with a smile.

Finally, after what seems like forever with both the men looking at me, I snap out of my slack-jaw stupor and say, "Commander, it's great to finally meet you. I'm so glad you could make it. Thank you for the recommendation for the academy. I'm certain it's why I got in."

He shakes his head, smile firmly in place. "No, kid. I saw your transcript. You got in because you worked hard. On the football field, in the classroom and in your community. The Naval

Academy is lucky to be getting such a well-rounded, hard-working young man. My letter was only a formality. You earned it."

I'm so glad my skin is darker and makes it harder to show the blush that I'm sure is spreading from my neck to my face. "Thank you, sir."

The Cheshire cat grin of pride hasn't left Judson's face. Before we can say anything else Lila returns from the bathroom with Quinn, squealing my name. When I turn and take a few steps to her she leaps up into my arms like she has springs on her feet. It's a good thing I lost the scrawny kid body somewhere along the way and packed on muscle as I grew taller or she'd knock me down when she jumps to me like this. I blow a raspberry on her cheek and listen to her laughter ring out in my ear.

Quinn leans in and asks, "Do you know who that is?"

"Yes, Commander Hayden. He's the guy who wrote my recommendation to the academy."

Quinn shares a wobbly smile and chokes out, "He's also the man who saved Judson's life."

"What?" I ask, confused. Judd never talks about the IED or what happened over there.

"Commander Hayden is the one who saved his life. Got pressure on the wound to slow the bleeding and carried him over a mile to help. Judson keeps in contact with him, called him for your recommendation but neither like to talk about it."

I stand there, stunned, reviewing what she's just shared with me. I just shook hands with the person responsible (in a roundabout way) for all that I have. As Judson is shaking the man's hand again and saying goodbye, I set Lila down and approach.

"Commander," I reach my hand out to his and grip tight when he takes it, "I'd like to thank you for...everything." I glance at Judson who's standing like stone looking at our clasped hands. "And I mean *everything*."

The commander pauses, his smile faltering as he gets my meaning. He returns the squeeze and says, "It was my pleasure."

I'm sure he understands what I'm trying to say. He releases my hand and strides away. I turn to face Judson and see for the first time in years, a vulnerable expression cross his features. I hug him and say, "thank you," low enough for only him to hear. He hates attention and accolades.

Pulling back just enough to keep half of the embrace, but close enough to keep the words between us, he says, "You helped to give me purpose. Our family gave me purpose and I've never been more proud in my life of anyone as I am of you."

Before we can get too choked up my friends hustle over to our group, horsing around and getting loud. Judson steps away from me as my boys pull me into their huddle, excitedly making plans for a wild night of celebration. As I glance up, I see Lila at his side, holding his hand as his lips meet Quincy's. I think to myself as I watch them. I want a love like that someday. One that makes me better, stronger, complete.

The End

For more information about upcoming releases, or to subscribe to Tiffani's newsletter, or contact her please visit her website www.tiffanilynn.com

ALSO BY TIFFANI LYNN

**You can find information on any of these books and how to contact Tiffani at www.Tiffanilynn.com.

Colorado Veterans Series

1. Finding Purpose

2. Finding Heart

3. Finding Passion

4. Finding Life

5. Finding Hope

Florida Veterans

1. Saving Summer

2. Saving Stacey

3. Saving Simone

4. Protecting Lucianna (Also part of Susan Stoker's Special Forces: Operation Alpha World

Betrayal to Bliss Series

1. Strangers at Sunset

2. From Strangers to Lovers

Eden's Odyssey Series

1. Finn's Shot (Free ebook)

2. Tangled with Tyler

MacGregor Family Novellas

1. Love, Lust & Life

2. Beauty, Bliss & A Bed of Roses

Stand Alone Novels

1. Rescuing Reya - Part of Elle James Brotherhood Protector World

50299850R00127